Sara Wood

HUSBAND BY ARRANGEMENT

Wedlocked!

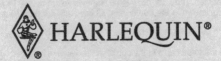

D0556987

HARLEQUIN®

TORONTO • NEW YORK • LONDON
AMSTERDAM • PARIS • SYDNEY • HAMBURG
STOCKHOLM • ATHENS • TOKYO • MILAN • MADRID
PRAGUE • WARSAW • BUDAPEST • AUCKLAND

If you purchased this book without a cover you should be aware that this book is stolen property. It was reported as "unsold and destroyed" to the publisher, and neither the author nor the publisher has received any payment for this "stripped book."

ISBN 0-373-12323-X

HUSBAND BY ARRANGEMENT

First North American Publication 2003.

Copyright © 2003 by Sara Wood.

All rights reserved. Except for use in any review, the reproduction or utilization of this work in whole or in part in any form by any electronic, mechanical or other means, now known or hereafter invented, including xerography, photocopying and recording, or in any information storage or retrieval system, is forbidden without the written permission of the publisher, Harlequin Enterprises Limited, 225 Duncan Mill Road, Don Mills, Ontario, Canada M3B 3K9.

All characters in this book have no existence outside the imagination of the author and have no relation whatsoever to anyone bearing the same name or names. They are not even distantly inspired by any individual known or unknown to the author, and all incidents are pure invention.

This edition published by arrangement with Harlequin Books S.A.

® and TM are trademarks of the publisher. Trademarks indicated with ® are registered in the United States Patent and Trademark Office, the Canadian Trade Marks Office and in other countries.

Visit us at www.eHarlequin.com

Printed in U.S.A.

"Let's be frank. Our grandparents have hopes of marriage between us, yes?"

"So I was led to believe," she hedged.

"Okay. To be honest, initially I didn't like the idea of being pushed into marriage with you," he told her.

"Thanks."

His eyes danced. And more. There was… admiration? Certainly desire. In buckets. She felt her body quiver.

"My pleasure," he said with a chuckle, nibbling her knuckles.

"So?" Stupid though it was, the feel of his mouth was robbing her of speech. Or perhaps it was the lowered flutter of his impossibly thick black lashes. "So," she said, appalled at how croaky she sounded. "What changed your mind?"

"You did."

He was croaky, too. Maddy began to panic. Dex wasn't supposed to be attracted to her!

"I did?" she squeaked in alarm.

"Very much so," he murmured. "You are…" His slow gaze burned all the way from the top of her head to her feet, stopping at strategic points in between. "A knockout," he said on a husky out-breath.

Legally wed,
But he's never said…
"I love you."

They're…

The series where marriages are made in haste…and love comes later…

Look out for more *Wedlocked!* stories in Harlequin Presents® throughout 2003.

Coming in July

Bride by Blackmail #2334
by
Carole Mortimer

CHAPTER ONE

MADDY had waited long enough. She had to see. Catching
her friend's hand in a desperate plea, she steeled herself for
the result.

'Let me look!' she begged.

Debbie laughed. 'Patience. Just a little more lipgloss....
There! Ready?'

Maddy nodded, her mouth horribly dry. So much rested
on this! The chair was swung around to face the mirror and
she found herself staring at a totally different person.

'Oh, my gosh!' she breathed in awe.

Instead of being outrageous, as she'd planned, the burgundy hair flattered her pale colouring and made her solemn grey eyes gleam with a smoky, almost wicked allure.
Her lips parted in astonishment and her poppy-coloured
mouth pouted back at her as if it were kissed forty times a
night.

As if! She smiled wryly. Since her last, barely-got-started
relationship had gone pear-shaped, her grandfather was the
only one who kissed her. On the cheek. And only to say
goodnight. Dear Grandpa, he didn't believe in displays of
affection, even though he did care for her.

That was why he was set on her marrying the grandson
of his ex-business partner in Portugal. And why she was
all done up like a dog's dinner—in a desperate effort to
look totally unsuitable as the future bride for Dexter
Fitzgerald. And why, in a few hours, she was flying out to
a country she'd left almost twenty years ago.

'It's a bit...over the top,' Maddy said doubtfully, shocked by the brazen hussy in the mirror.

''Course it is. How else are you to be rejected point-blank? You said the Fitzgeralds were traditional-minded. Trust me. They'll be appalled.'

Maddy began to smile. Her hopes rose.

'I think they might!' she conceded.

'Now you've got to learn to do a come-hither walk,' commanded Debbie. 'Like *this*.'

Egged on by her giggling friend, Maddy leapt from the chair and followed Debbie, exaggerating the swing of her leather-clad hips till she felt her pelvis would break loose from its moorings.

'It's too ridiculous!' she protested, as they fell in a heap of helpless laughter on her friend's bed. 'I could never walk like that in public!'

'Duckie, you've got to overdo it if you're to succeed. That's why we bought the gaudiest clothes from the charity shop.' Debbie's face grew serious. 'Look, you have no choice. Your grandfather's been on and on at you for ages. He's mad keen for you to marry this Dexter guy. This will definitely foil his plans.'

'He wants me to be secure,' she defended loyally. 'He thinks I'm a hopeless case because I'm thirty. *And* I'm un-employed, now that the children's home has closed. I'm going to miss working there,' she sighed. 'But you can understand his concern. He's old and sick and worried what'll happen when he dies.'

Debbie sniffed. 'Personally, I'd tell my grandpa to stay out of my life.' Her face softened and she hugged Maddy warmly. 'Trouble is, being the kind, caring person you are, you're trying not to upset him. So here you are, apparently submissive and on the brink of flying to Portugal to meet your eager bridegroom and—'

'Hell-bent on behaving like a badly behaved gold-digger to put him off!' Maddy giggled, batting her eyes like mad.

'Brilliant! You can do it!' crowed Debbie.

'Can I?'

'Sure! Psyche yourself up. Look at yourself!' encouraged Debbie.

She dragged Maddy back to the mirror. Fiddling with her alarmingly low-cut top, Maddy thought of the prim and grim Sofia Fitzgerald, Dex's grandmother. Sofia would loathe a money-grabbing vamp as a prospective bride for Dex—and from what she remembered of him, he'd want a docile, nicely dressed woman to be his wife, not a flighty-looking piece with a come-hither walk.

Maddy pushed back her uncertainties. It would be the act of a lifetime. But her grandfather had been almost apoplectic when she'd tried to tell him she didn't want to go along with his marriage plans. If she wanted to stop her grandfather from having another heart attack, she had no choice. She'd appear to go along with his plan, but would make sure it failed. She took a deep breath and summoned up all her inner strength.

'Then help me, Debs,' she said decisively. 'Teach me what to do.'

They practised being sensual, bold and assertive. Took a walk outside, drawing lustful glances. Amidst the laughter she shared with her friend, Maddy found herself gaining in confidence as the day wore on and she was being openly propositioned in the street.

Now she was the kind of woman that men picked up! It still felt very unnatural to her, but at least she could *pretend* to be a sex-siren, if only for a short while. She would appear to be totally unsuitable as a Fitzgerald bride. The marriage-making that had gone on between Maddy's grandfather and the aristocratic Sofia would come to nothing.

'Just don't be your usual sweet self. You're a sharp cookie, remember,' Debbie warned as she finally drove Maddy to the airport.

'Dex would hate that,' Maddy mused. 'I didn't see him very often after his eighth birthday when he went to boarding-school in England, and I was only four at the time. But I remember he was very reclusive and aloof—'

'With bottleglass specs and as thin as a reed,' Debbie reminded her.

'I'm sure he's very nice,' Maddy conceded kindly, twiddling a spiky piece of hair. 'But I'd never marry someone I didn't love.'

Her husband would have to be very understanding, she thought. Her restless hands stilled. Someone who didn't mind that she couldn't have children. She had come to terms with that a long time ago, after the infection had ruined her chances of motherhood, even though the inner ache, the wistful longing, would be with her always. What man would be content with just her, and no child to call his own?

'You're pretty tough, aren't you? Even though you might seem quiet and submissive to people who don't know you,' Debbie said admiringly. 'I don't know how you've coped, being head cook and bottle-washer to your grandfather all these years. He's a bit of a tyrant, isn't he?'

'He needed me,' Maddy said simply. 'And I learnt to keep quiet and get on with things when the business he started up over here failed and we lost all our money.'

'Rotten for you.'

'Worse for him.' She remembered how hard it had been for her grandfather to be poor. The Fitzgeralds had settled a large sum on him in exchange for his share of the plant nursery in Portugal. But all of that money had been swallowed up by debts. 'If only Grandpa didn't feel such a violent resentment towards the Fitzgerald family!' she sighed. 'He thinks that half of Dex's inheritance should rightly be mine. That's why he's so determined that the two of us should marry.'

Debbie looked puzzled. 'Why does he resent the Fitzgerald millions?'

Maddy fell silent for a moment. 'He blames them for the car accident that caused the deaths of my parents and Dex's,' she explained sadly. 'Our two families shared the same rambling farmhouse in Portugal. Apparently Dex's mother flung herself at my father. If she hadn't, Grandpa says, there would have been no accident whatsoever. We'd be wealthy, both sets of parents would be alive and we'd all still live in Portugal.'

'Can't dwell in the past,' Debbie said, matter-of-fact as ever. 'You've got a future to plan. Almost there. Remember: stay in character. Do things that are socially unacceptable.'

Squaring her shoulders, Maddy resolutely faced up to the challenge ahead.

'Like slurping my soup?' she suggested.

The car rolled to a stop. 'Perfect. Or do the cancan on the table. Eat spaghetti with your fingers. Anything. Just come back single!'

Maddy slid out, moving carefully to keep her balance in the gold killer heels. Two male passers-by leapt over to help her with her luggage and she beamed her thanks at them. Their eyes glazed over and she saw Debbie giving her a conspiratorial wink.

'Go for it,' her friend said fondly, hugging her. 'Show time! Have fun.'

'I will!'

Maddy felt excited. She'd quickly scotch any ideas of a

loveless marriage and then demand to hear the Fitzgeralds' version of the events leading to the fatal car accident.

However hard she'd probed, her grandfather had refused to explain why her loving father had run off with Dex's mother without saying goodbye. There had to be a good reason—and this was her opportunity to discover it.

Her eyes sparkled. For once in her life, she had a wonderful sense of taking control of her own life. It was exhilarating to feel so free.

With a wave to her approving friend, she graciously allowed one of the young men to push the luggage trolley and set off after him, her hips swinging exuberantly in the tight leather skirt.

This was an adventure, she thought. And she was determined to enjoy it.

CHAPTER TWO

DEXTER'S manic schedule meant that he'd come to the airport grimy and unshaven. Sourly he waited as the passengers from the London flight filed past, though he barely saw them, not even the admiring glances from women as they passed.

His mind was elsewhere: on the charred ruins of the Quinta, that had once been the Fitzgerald home.

He didn't want to be here. Hell, he didn't even want to be in the country.

Seeing a plump, timid-looking woman in ill-fitting clothes, he raised his placard with exhausted resignation. She caught his eye, brightened and then looked at the hastily felt-tipped name: Maddy Cook. Looking disappointed, the woman continued dolefully on her way through Faro Airport. Not her, then.

The last stragglers wandered out and he was on his own. It seemed that Maddy wasn't coming to the Algarve after all, and he felt such a huge sense of relief that he might have burst into song if he hadn't been so dog-tired and disinclined for anything remotely resembling merriment.

Then, just as he turned to leave, his attention was caught by a crowd of chattering, laughing men who'd surged through from Customs. Dexter saw that they were rugby players on tour, complete with team kit, coach, acolytes and, he noted appreciatively, a team mascot.

The mascot's burgundy head bobbed up and down amid the ruck, almost lost under the welter of burly arms and giant hands. But between the mountainous shoulders and

11

tree-trunk thighs Dex had glimpsed her dazzling grin and stunning legs. For the first time in a week his stony face cracked with the faint hint of a smile.

'Hey, babe, here's your meeter-and-greeter!' shouted one of the giants, pointing directly at him.

Dex turned around, expecting to see—somewhere behind him—a welcoming committee of seven-foot giants in striped jerseys bulging with muscles. He saw nothing of the kind.

And when he turned back he noticed that the scrum had parted to reveal the mascot in all her glory. Despite his hurry to leave, he paused, utterly arrested by the startling sight.

She was like an exotic butterfly, shimmering with glitter and iridescence. Obvious, for sure. Not his type. Yet something about her joyous exuberance and lovely face touched his rock-bottom spirits and lifted the weight that had settled so leadenly in his mind.

He blinked. The butterfly was coming in his direction, her smoky eyes fixed with eager interest on the placard he was still holding.

His mouth dried. It couldn't be. Wrong shape. Wrong personality...

'Hi,' she said breathily. 'I'm Maddy. Are you the driver?'

Maddy? He stared. Impossible! And yet there were the enormous grey eyes, though they were sparkling instead of how he remembered them—apprehensive and all too ready to shed tears.

There was something vaguely familiar in that mouth, too, even if the fine cheekbones and delicately shaped nose bore no resemblance to the podgy, childish features he remembered.

'You are my driver?' she prompted with an extraordinarily sweet smile, enunciating clearly and making steering motions with her hands.

'Uh,' he said inadequately, wondering how anyone short, plump and permanently anxious could ever have hatched into this extraordinary, confident bombshell of a woman.

She put her head on one side and looked uncertain.

'Oh, dear. You've no idea what I'm saying, have you? My Portuguese is horribly rusty. Do you speak any English?' she asked with slow care.

He'd thought that nothing could surprise him any more. He'd travelled the world. Been startled, shocked and scared out of his wits. One broken arm, several broken ribs and a snake-bite to show for his travels. Two passionate affairs, a wonderful but poignantly brief marriage, his bride dead of dengue fever before their unborn child could survive outside the womb. His mouth tightened and he forced back the desperately painful memory.

Perhaps because he put himself in dangerous situations, life was always flinging him off balance. And it had done it again.

This was an amazing transformation. Tubby little Maddy. To *this*! He rubbed a hand over his stubbled jaw in amazement.

'English. Er—yeah,' he managed, and she nodded, bright with relief, then wiggled her way back to the rugby players, blissfully unaware of Dexter's confusion. He found that his jaw had dropped open and hastily closed it.

Ironically, she hadn't recognised him at all. Though of course he'd changed considerably since his skinny youth. That could be to his advantage. Could he keep his identity a secret? His mind whirled with possibilities.

He'd been expecting the dullest, dreariest woman alive. After all, Maddy had been brought up by her tyrannical old grandfather and was still living with him. He'd imagined that she'd only survive such a relationship if she was subservient and obedient.

He'd believed that she had meekly obeyed her grandfather's command to put herself up for marriage because she was too scared to disobey. In other words, he'd been convinced she must be a doormat.

This Maddy, however, would be *on* the doormat, wiping her feet on others. It didn't make sense.

He appraised her body and her manner. Spectacular. Flirtatious. Confused, he drew in a sharp breath as something else occurred to him. By no means was this a timid granddaughter who was doing old man Cook's bidding. She was assertive enough to know exactly what she was getting into.

His eyes narrowed. That meant she really *wanted* to be a bride to the Fitzgerald heir! The mercenary little minx!

Well, he'd soon put her straight about her chances. He'd only agreed to meet her at the airport because his grandmother wouldn't get off his back about this getting married business. Apparently she'd had a crisis of conscience, now that old man Cook was in poor health and Maddy was likely to be left a pauper when he died.

Dex was far too busy to dance attendance on a woman. But he'd been sure that his grandmother would forget her desire to marry him off when she saw how unsuitable the dull, meek little Maddy was—and when he made it clear that he had no interest whatsoever in his proposed boring little bride.

With a flash of amusement, it occurred to him that Maddy *was* unsuitable—but in a totally unexpected way! This seductive little madam might make men's eyes come out on stalks, but she'd horrify his grandmother.

He relaxed. He'd be off the hook. What a relief.

Dazed, he watched the men bending to kiss Maddy farewell, her slender, luscious body dwarfed by so much muscle and brawn. One solid head after another dipped gently towards hers. There were promises of meetings; she was going to watch them play; they were going to treat her to a slap-up meal.

And then they were gone in a rush of testosterone and body odour and Maddy was dashing up to him again, bodice glittering, eyes as bright as diamonds.

Hell. He nearly smiled at her infectious enthusiasm.

'Hope you don't mind,' she apologised. 'Had to say goodbye. They were so sweet to me on the flight. Sorry if you've been waiting long,' she breathed happily, flushed and flashing a friendly grin at him.

Her extraordinary hair was tousled and there was such an air of sensuality about her that she looked as if she'd been recently hauled away from a particularly energetic orgy.

Dexter tried to keep his scowl going but it was hard. He felt as if all the darkness that inhabited his body had been lit up by an arc lamp. But he couldn't let himself be diverted. There were far more important things on his mind.

'I'd given you up,' he muttered, his voice hoarse from the inhalation of the dust and smoke he'd been working with all day.

He had already focused again on the matter that had occupied his mind and body for the past week: the wreckage of his old family home. Or what had once been a home.

His mouth tightened into a grim line and his features settled into a heavy frown. He was impatient to get back, get things done.

'Oh, dear. You do look cross! It wasn't my fault, though. The fact is, I was searched!' she cried, grey eyes all wide and astonished. 'Every scrap of my luggage—and almost *me*! I've heard what they do and I was scared, I can tell you. Now, give me your honest opinion. Do I look as if I'm a drug addict?' she asked indignantly.

Reeling from her chatter, he checked, working his way up and down. Her glittering gold top seemed to be wrestling with her breasts, which were making a bid for freedom. They were unnervingly close to succeeding.

Suddenly he realised to his horror that he'd started to sizzle with a vital energy, the blood roaring around his veins as if it were racing to reach his heart to win a prize.

He scowled. She was certainly altering his body functions. He supposed it was a long time since he'd been even vaguely interested in a woman and he wished his hormones hadn't chosen this particular moment in time to make themselves known.

But the curves of her lush figure literally took his breath away. To say nothing of the tight leather skirt and slender legs which went on forever and which were causing a glow to spread in the direction of his loins.

Feeling irritable with himself, he answered her query with a shrug and assumed cynically that the officials had just wanted to keep her in their sights as long as possible.

'Perhaps they thought you were on amphetamines. Some kind of stimulant,' he suggested.

'The only stimulants I've had in the past twenty-four hours are coffee and *life*.' She giggled, spread her arms wide as if to embrace everybody within reach. 'And that's more than enough for me!'

'Shall we go?' he groused, wondering why she was so all-fired happy.

Maddy looked at him from under her lashes, trying very hard to look coquettish.

'Let's. But would you be a sweetie and push my trolley?' she chirruped. 'It keeps going left when I'm heading right and I lurch into people. Some like that, some don't, and

I'd rather not upset anyone.' She flashed him an enormous smile and virtually purred, 'You look strong enough to control it.'

His mouth tightened. Typical of the female burble he loathed. Flatter a man, twist him around your little finger, suck his bank balance dry. He'd met plenty of those in his lifetime.

And yet her admiring glance had apparently hit the spot. His pulses were racing madly.

Disgusted that his body had, like the trolley, developed a mind of its own, he took charge of the waywardly swerving luggage.

And there on the top of it all he noticed a book entitled *How to Catch Your Man*. Beneath that chilling title were the words *and Make Him Marry You*.

His stomach muscles clenched with horror and any passing interest in Maddy suddenly ceased.

'This way,' he growled, intent on getting rid of the threat to his freedom as fast as possible.

She beamed. 'Right. Take me to your leader. I can't wait to meet him!'

He grunted. Blithely Maddy sashayed along beside him. Dexter quickly realised that the whole airport was grinding to a halt around her. People were grinning, staring, commenting. Men openly lusted. Women looked sour and made catty comments behind their hands.

And she swayed on regardless, her walk uncomfortably reminiscent of Marilyn Monroe in *Some Like it Hot*.

Dexter surreptitiously ran a finger around his collar, thinking that the temperature had certainly risen a few degrees since she'd arrived.

'You know, you look a bit like Dexter,' she ventured. He started, and she must have thought he was insulted by the comparison, because she said with a placatory haste,

'Only fleetingly. Just something about the eyes. I doubt he's as—er—well-built as you. Do you work for the Fitzgerald family?' she asked breathily, apparently mesmerised by the sooty streaks across his chest.

Presumably she was finding it hard to breathe because she was having difficulty keeping up. For some reason, his stride seemed to have increased to a half-jog.

Easing up, he tried a noncommittal, 'Uh,' still toying with the idea of pretending to be someone else.

'You haven't told me your name,' she encouraged.

'Nope.'

She waited but he didn't elaborate. He wanted to keep conversation to a minimum. That way he could hang on to his dignity and not start panting like a dog on heat.

Stealing a sideways glance at Maddy, he saw that some of the bounce had gone out of her—though he doubted that had anything to do with him. A woman who was this confident wouldn't be bothered in the least if she was snubbed by a grubby driver in a cinder-stained T-shirt and torn jeans.

Gloom settled over him again. He was filthy because he was working night and day, eating on the run and even occasionally crashing out in the smoking ruins of the Quinta.

Whenever he closed his eyes, all he saw were the charred timbers and scorched earth. His mind constantly raced with the thousand and one things he had to do. When he slept he dreamed of fire consuming whole forests. When he woke the images of desolation became reality.

His head was perpetually filled with the consequences of the disaster. The disruption to his life. His enforced return to Portugal. The destruction of thousands of valuable stock plants in the nursery and the knowledge that he was the only person who could build the business up again.

The forest fire had devoured several thousand acres of eucalyptus trees around the Fitzgerald estate. It had swept on to the eighteenth century manor house, the Quinta, which had been in its path. The majority of their land had been laid to waste and his distraught grandmother had summoned him from Brazil to recreate the farm and the nursery-garden business from the ashes.

Of course he'd agreed to come. Whatever had divided them before, his grandmama was elderly and she needed him.

But he felt trapped. Missed his travels. The joy of plant hunting, obtaining permissions for propagation and seed collection, organising production and despatch. A life of freedom and independence. The life he had chosen when his beloved mother had deserted him for Maddy's father, Jim Cook, when his safe haven had suddenly become cold and unwelcoming.

Wretched with grief after the terrible accident had wiped out his parents and Maddy's, he'd turned his back on everything he'd once loved. He didn't miss his macho, authoritarian father, who'd made it no secret that a reserved, myopic son had been a disappointment. But his mother had loved him for his kind heart and his passion for plants. Until Jim Cook had turned her head.

If it hadn't been for the fire, he wouldn't be here. His grandmother wouldn't have nagged him about producing an heir. And he wouldn't be fending off the avaricious daughter of the man who'd seduced his mother and enticed her away…

He stopped himself from thinking further. Too painful.

Anger surged through him. His jaw tightened and his dark eyes glittered with loathing. The last person on earth he'd marry was the daughter of Jim Cook.

Even before he'd met her, he'd decided to make her feel

completely unwelcome. Ensure that her stay was unpleasant. And he knew just how he could do that. By the time he'd finished with her she'd be hitching a lift back to the airport and taking the next plane home.

He wasn't going to marry anyone from the Cook family. Especially a gold-digger. More important, he wasn't ever going to *marry* again. Full stop.

CHAPTER THREE

GRIMLY plotting mayhem, Dexter lobbed Maddy's luggage with studied carelessness into the back of the pick-up, on top of the equipment he'd collected from the builders' yard.

'Gosh,' she said, with an appealingly infectious giggle. 'You could get work as a baggage handler any day.'

Dex met her amused glance with a blank stare. Privately he'd expected Maddy to have changed—but not this much! Maddy had rarely spoken unless given permission by her bullying grandfather.

Old man Cook had ruled his family like a dictator. For the first time it occurred to him that this might be why Maddy's gentle, plant-loving father might have wanted to escape the evil old tyrant's influence.

'Get in,' he said curtly.

Just in time, he remembered not to open the door for her, or to offer to help her up the high step. He had to give her the maximum of aggravation. And in that skirt she had a serious handicap, he thought with malicious satisfaction.

'This'll be fun. I've never been in a pick-up before!' she declared enthusiastically. 'Right.' She took a deep breath that threatened the fragile construction of her straining top. 'Here we go. Avert your eyes.'

He did nothing of the kind. Sourly he watched while she hitched up her soft leather skirt to eye-blinking heights, slipped off her spiky shoes and hauled herself onto the first step.

Perfect thighs. Toned and firm and clearly the result of high-maintenance work-outs in the gym. Cynically he saw her wrench open the buckled door a few inches and virtually limbo-dance her way in through its reluctant gap.

He couldn't believe that Maddy could be so uninhibited. Or assertive. But he steeled himself not to show his grudging admiration.

'Crikey! It's very dirty in here,' she commented, when he clambered into the driver's seat beside her.

Illogically it annoyed him that she was stating a fact and didn't seem in the least bit put out by the mode of transport, or its ramshackle nature.

'Been too close to a fire,' was all he offered, starting up the engine.

'Oh. Camp?'

'No. I'm straight,' he replied, deliberately misinterpreting her.

She gave a little gurgle of laughter.

'I mean was it a camp fire?'

'Forest.'

'Were you in it?'

'The forest or truck?' he drawled, annoyed to be enjoying the exchange.

'Truck!' She laughed in delight.

'No.'

'Lucky for you,' she said, sounding surprisingly heartfelt.

Other than that, she made no comment about the fire. He assumed that was because his grandmother had already warned old man Cook about it—and also reassured him that the Fitzgerald wealth could easily weather the disaster.

Dexter's mouth grew cynical. Maddy had come, even though she'd known she'd be making do in a small cottage on the estate. She must be desperate to marry a fortune!

Breaking the silence that had fallen, she sighed and shot

all his nerves to pieces by stretching wantonly in a flurry of sensual limbs and writhing curves.

'I'm absolutely shattered,' she confided. 'Don't be surprised if I fall asleep on the journey. No criticism of your conversational skills. It's tiring being on show,' she added absently.

What the devil did she mean by that? He frowned and deliberately drove fast over the humps in the road in an effort to get back as quickly as possible. But behind them the scaffolding clanged up and down in metallic protest and she let out a squeal.

Mistakenly he flicked a quick look at her and then concentrated fiercely on the road again. Unfortunately his vision retained the image of two firm, flawless breasts quivering seductively as the truck bounced over the uneven surface. And his body responded with the kind of enthusiasm that any self-respecting male would expect.

'Sit tight,' he growled irritably. 'This truck isn't designed for women.'

'You can say that again. My bits are going everywhere. So why did Dexter send it for me?' she demanded, yanking up her bodice indignantly.

'I was coming to Faro for supplies,' he clipped, annoyingly unable to forget the alluring sight of her 'bits'. 'No point in two vehicles making the journey. Takes two hours to the Quinta.'

She groaned. 'My bones'll be jumbled into a completely different person if we go on like this! If you don't want to end up with a Quasimodo next to you, I suggest you attack the bumps with less vigour.'

He intended to do just that. His libido was giving him enough trouble as it was, without witnessing another seismic shift of her body.

'Got to hurry. Get back to work,' he muttered in excuse.

'Doing what?'

'This and that.'

For a moment she looked floored by his reticence, then gamely started the conversation again.

'I used to live here, you know.'

'Mmm.'

As sure as hell, he wasn't going to encourage reminiscences.

'Yes,' she said, undeterred. 'My grandfather and Dexter's grandfather set up the garden centre together. They'd been friends since childhood and chose to go out to Portugal because it was an up-and-coming place for ex-pats to settle,' she told him, and paused for his comment.

Hoping his silence would shut her up, he just glared at the road. Annoyingly she launched off again, clearly in a chatty mood.

'Grandpa was the business brain, Mr Fitzgerald was the plantsman. They married Portuguese women. So did my father, so I have Portuguese blood,' she announced. 'I was born on the farm, like Dexter. I was there for the first eleven years of my life.'

'Really?'

He didn't want to think about it. Unfortunately she ignored his plainly uninterested comment and forged on, opening old wounds, old memories.

'Mmm. Our two families lived together because it was cheaper than running two houses and they could put more money into the actual business. I suppose it was more convenient, too. Not so far to commute.'

She went quiet for a moment and he shifted uncomfortably. There had always been tensions between the two grandfathers. One saw the Quinta purely as a commercial venture, the other as a wonderful way of life.

'My grandpa says Mr Fitzgerald senior died a year or so ago.'

'Yes.'

She wasn't put off by his curtness. 'I liked him. Those were the days,' she continued dreamily. 'We all mucked in together at the Quinta. Not much money, but bags of hope and mega-size dreams—built on the back of the new villa developments in the Algarve which needed their gardens landscaped. We were two close families, working all hours to build up the business.'

Close families! Too damn close. Grimly he turned on the radio, not wanting to hear any more. He had enough to deal with. Memories could stay where they were.

'You're very grumpy. I thought you'd be interested,' she said, sounding hurt.

He snorted but didn't reply. Privately crushed by his abruptness, Maddy watched him scowling at the road ahead as if it deserved his revenge.

And yet despite his sullen, antisocial manner, he was quite a dish in a basic kind of way: tall, well-built and undeniably handsome.

The smell of smoke hung around him and he clearly hadn't washed his clothes for days or cleaned his finger-nails. His hands were ingrained with dirt and there were streaks of black decorating his broad forehead and strong cheekbones. Even his voice sounded husky, as if he'd chain-smoked all his life.

But his profile was to die for: a dark and brooding eye beneath a lowered black brow, the firm jut of a nose and a chiselled mouth that Michelangelo would have been proud to have created. Though, she mused, Michelangelo might have stopped short at the designer stubble, however sexy it looked.

This was a true labouring man, she decided. Rough and

ready. No conversationalist. And yet passion lurked in those dark eyes. Pity Dex couldn't be more like him instead of detached and distant. Thinking of their imminent meeting, she shuddered with apprehension.

'If you're cold, there's a sack in the back you could put over your shoulders,' he suggested sardonically.

Her mouth twitched at the caveman offer and, thinking of Debbie's instructions to stay in character, she raked up a reply to suit her personality.

'A sack? *Moi?* I'd rather freeze,' she said with a giggle and, in the absence of a decent chat, opened her book on getting her man for some quick revision.

The truck suddenly lurched forwards and she struggled to find her place as the Hunk hurtled along the motorway with scant regard for the suspension—either the truck's or hers.

All she needed to do, she reminded herself, dismissing her grumpy companion for more important things, was to make sure her behaviour was the exact opposite of what the book advised.

She mustn't be a woman with wife potential. She had to be a 'good for now' kind of girl. That was a task she felt was within her grasp, since she'd practised on the rugby team. They'd been hugely appreciative and their delight in her company had given her confidence a huge boost.

It had been fun, too. The most fun she'd had *ever*. Nothing heavy, just wall-to-wall flirting and endless laughter. All perfectly harmless.

Frowning with concentration, she delved into the chapter on how to charm a man with sweetness and submission. Always agree, always defer. Hmm.

Her eyes gleamed as she planned her tactics on going completely against her character and doing nothing of the kind.

By putting a spanner in the attempted matchmaking, she was only being kind. Her subterfuge was all for the best. Dexter needed a battleaxe of a wife who'd stand up to his domineering grandmother.

Maddy smiled wryly to herself. Just as she needed a gritty, assertive husband who wouldn't shake like a jelly when he met her stern grandfather.

None of her boyfriends had stood the Grandpa test. They had all run a mile at his first bark and hadn't even made it to his bite. But they'd been pretty lacklustre, if she was honest.

Her face grew wistful. When would a gorgeous, independent cuss of a man ever look twice at a mouse like her? Of course, she could probably lure a guy who fell for her brassy, extrovert image, but where would that get her? She was really quiet and shy. Would she want to live a lie for the rest of her life?

She checked her useless thoughts. This was ridiculous! It was silly to even contemplate the idea of marriage. It would never happen.

Sadly she closed the book, the corners of her bright mouth drooping. She wanted to be someone's wife. Wanted babies, loads and loads of them. Like her friends, who seemed to be forever swelling or giving birth or pushing buggies and wailing about sleepless nights. But she couldn't have children and that was that. She knew the score.

Her hand came to rest on her abdomen. Her mouth tightened in suppressed anguish as she remembered vividly the agony of the infection which had ruined her chances of motherhood some ten years earlier, when she was just twenty.

Despite her efforts, she couldn't stop herself reliving

those mind-numbing moments when the doctor had sat on the end of her bed and sympathetically said…

'Feel all right?' asked the Hunk abruptly.

She jerked and hastily drew her hand away, startled that he'd noticed her mournful expression. She'd thought he'd been intent on glaring the road into abject submission.

'OK,' she mumbled unconvincingly, unable to lift the dullness of her voice.

Unexpected tears welled up in her eyes. Over the years she'd had to accept the fact that she'd never have a child, but somehow coming to Portugal had unsettled her emotions.

Her teeth clamped together as she tried to crush her useless, destructive thoughts. But she would have given anything to have a baby. Anything.

Without comment, he swerved to the inside lane and took an exit which led them to a small, bustling village. Struggling fiercely with her stupidly wayward emotions, Maddy didn't recognise it at all but was too choked up to ask what he was doing.

And yet there was something calming about the twisty cobbled roads lined with crumbling white houses. The village clearly was a poor one, but roses trailed around the wonky wooden doors and geraniums tumbled down from pots on rickety balconies.

Everything came flooding back to her. This was the old Portugal, the one she'd known as a child, and far more recognisable than the smart motorway and huge villa developments they'd passed so far.

Trundling beneath the lines of washing which hung across the street, the truck finally stopped in a small square surrounded by orange trees. A wonderful silence descended, broken only by the sound of birdsong. It was heavenly.

The truck driver turned to her and scowled. 'Out!'

Grimly he walked around and jerked at her door, the metal screeching in protest as his brute strength levered the door completely open.

She stared at his unfriendly face in dismay as it became apparent that he wasn't intending to have a potentially weepy woman in the cab and had decided to abandon her, then and there.

He pinned her with his cold and uncompromising stare. And then anger gave her the courage to fling herself in the direction of the driver's seat. For a moment she found herself intimately linked with the gear stick and then she was tumbling into place and switching on the ignition.

Which was just as quickly switched off by a large, warm hand which clamped down on hers and deftly twisted her fingers in an anticlockwise direction till the engine died.

'What do you think you're doing?' he enquired, his deep, throaty voice somewhere in the region of her right ear.

'Isn't it obvious?' she husked, suddenly swamped, it seemed, by the smell of smoke and warm, body-tingling man.

'Do you know how to drive a truck?' he growled.

'No, I don't!'

'Then why try?' he asked, not unreasonably.

Her stormy eyes flashed angrily to his. His face was close, invading her personal space. Trying not to be intimidated, she said, 'It was me or you and I chose me!'

His forehead furrowed. 'What?'

'You were going to dump me by the road!' she cried hotly.

He looked exasperated. 'Don't be ridiculous. I was going to take you into that bar for a coffee or a brandy.'

Startled, she jerked her head around to peer at the building behind him. There was, indeed, a bar.

'Why?' she asked, utterly confused.

Only inches away, the dark eyes bored into hers without compassion or sympathy. She felt suddenly weak, blasted by his intense masculinity.

'You're tired. Or upset. It doesn't matter which,' he muttered gruffly. 'It was all I could think of.'

'Oh!' She moved back to escape his compelling power. Her brain began to work and as it did her anger subsided. He was being kind in his curt, funny way! She smiled gratefully. 'Sorry. My mistake. That's very thoughtful. Thanks. I would like a coffee.'

He narrowed his eyes and considered her with care. The scrutiny caused a *frisson* to ripple through her, taking her unawares. But then few gorgeous men ever paid her any attention normally, she reasoned. And decided that it was all very unsettling.

'Would you really have driven away and left me here?' he murmured, obviously intrigued.

'Yes, of course!' she declared, still a little amazed at her own nerve. 'How else would I get to the Quinta?'

He let out a bark of surprised laughter and then hastily stifled it as if it was something forbidden. Then he swung himself out again, onto the step.

'I think,' he said in steel-trap tones, 'I need a brandy.'

For a moment she lowered her eyes in feminine acquiescence of male rights, before she remembered who she was and blurted out her initial thought.

'Good grief! Your driving's energetic enough without it being fuelled by alcohol!' she reproved daringly.

He stepped down. 'I'm taking a lunch break,' he drawled. 'I intend to soak up the brandy with a large plate of fresh, chargrilled sardines on *pão integral*.'

'Local bread,' she remembered wistfully, her mouth watering as she recalled the enormous, tasty sardines on chunks of rough wholemeal. 'That sounds wonderful. I'll join you.'

Grabbing her shoes in one hand, she began to clamber out, and found herself stuck on the lower step above a large puddle, just where she'd land if she jumped down. She noticed then that the leather of the truck driver's working boots were stained with water where he'd already walked through the puddle.

So she waved her bare feet at him and smiled expectantly. He did nothing. Just stood back and watched her, hatchet-faced and ungallant. Sir Walter Raleigh he was *not*.

Just as she was resigning herself to an impromptu paddle in what might be sewage for all she knew, a group of males appeared as if from nowhere. They were unshaven and grinning, all ages from teens to nineties, and clearly encouraging her to leap into their arms.

She dithered, feeling both flustered and touched by their concern. 'Oh, you're very kind. I don't—'

Two firm hands came to settle around her waist. Before she could protest, she was being lifted into the air as the truck driver swung her up and over the puddle then deposited her safely on a strip of grass.

'Thanks!' she husked, stooping to slip her shoes on and going pink from the interest caused when she bent down.

Oddly, she felt dizzy and disorientated, and she didn't know if it was from the driver's intense masculinity or because she hadn't eaten for hours. Probably both. And the swooping sensation had been due to being lifted and deposited rather quickly. A kind of inner-ear problem.

'Come on,' he muttered.

Meekly she followed his broad back. Patently unwilling to miss the entertainment on offer, the village men swept into the bar behind them. They sat close by, raising their glasses to her and looking openly admiring.

There was an audible, communal sigh when she unthinkingly crossed one leg over the other, forgetting she was wearing something tight, short and revealing, instead of her usual grey and shapeless skirt.

'I'm going to the washroom. I'll put in our order on the way,' the truck driver said curtly.

'Oh,' she whispered, suddenly nervous. 'Don't leave me! I feel like an exhibit.'

He grunted. 'You ask to be ogled, wearing those clothes,' he told her heartlessly. 'And I'm not eating till I've washed.'

He had some standards, then. She watched him stride to the counter, and felt sympathy for the starry-eyed waitress who could hardly keep her eyes off the ultimate alpha male who was growling out his order as if it were a request for a suicide pill instead of sardines.

Rehearsing her role as a shameless hussy, Maddy studied him boldly. The muscles in his back rippled wonderfully when he moved. His rear was small and tight and he walked as if he was used to the freedom of the open air.

A wicked thought came into her head. Suppose, when she was talking to Sofia, she let slip that she was wildly attracted to the company's truck driver?

With a giggle of horror at her audacity, she mulled this over while the man in question freshened up. A few minutes later the door to the men's room opened and she hastily pretended to be studying her book again.

The hairs on the back of her neck tingled. She heard the firm stride of those heavy boots, the scrape of the chair opposite her as it was pulled to the table and then the faint smell of soap wafted to her nostrils.

She kept on reading, absently threading her hands through her hair until she was aware of a lot of deep breathing from the men around her.

'You trying to be provocative?' muttered the driver crossly.

She let her arms drop and bit back an indignant no. It would be safer to stay in character. Her behaviour might be reported back to the family. She racked her brains for what a siren might say.

'No, I'm not trying. Comes naturally,' she cooed.

He looked down his nose at her in disgust.

'Unlike your hair colour.'

She smiled and batted her eyelashes in response.

'Do you think it suits me?' she asked coyly.

And, to her astonishment, she found herself holding her breath, hoping he did.

'You'd look better blonde,' was his laconic verdict.

Her natural colour! She decided to be blunt in return. He'd clearly scrubbed his hands and had tried to brush the dust out of his hair but he still looked grubby.

'Why don't you bother to keep yourself clean?' she ventured curiously.

His frown deepened, the hard line of his mouth unutterably grim.

'Don't have time. Stopped work, drove to Faro, rushed to the builders' yard, then the airport.'

'You could have set the alarm earlier,' she said, realising to her horror that she was unconsciously echoing her grandfather.

Before she could apologise profusely, she saw that the dark eyes suddenly looked tired and that there was a deeper tightening of the muscles around his mouth.

'Four o'clock's early enough for me,' he growled.

'Four…!' She planted her hands on her hips indignantly, faintly conscious of a swell in the murmuring of the village men around them as she did so. But she was annoyed with the autocratic Fitzgeralds for taking advantage of their employee. 'That's outrageous!' she declared hotly, totally forgetting who she was supposed to be. 'I'll speak to Dexter and tell him to stop exploiting you—'

'You'll be wasting your time. I have to get through the work somehow,' he said tersely.

Her tender heart was touched. She imagined that he had a family to support. A dark-haired wife—very pretty but careworn—and four children, she imagined. Perhaps a widowed mother.

'I must do something!' she declared anxiously.

He frowned excessively. 'Maddy—'

'Sardinhas, aguardiente.'

The barman put two huge plates in front of them and a tot of rough brandy which she knew was strong enough to strip paint.

She felt disappointed. It had seemed for a moment that the truck driver was going to confide in her. Instead, he belligerently tucked into the sardines, not even looking up when the barman brought her coffee and a bottle of water.

It didn't matter, she thought sympathetically, watching the driver decapitate the first sardine with the skill of an executioner. She'd take up his cause, even if he *didn't* have a wife and kids.

Her expression grew sad again and she attacked the fish, doggedly determined to blank out the thought that she would never have a family of her own.

'What's the matter?' he asked irritably.

Furious with her uncharacteristic self-pity, she kept her head down and scowled. What was the matter with her? Being in Portugal had really unleashed her emotions! 'Nothing,' she muttered, munching suddenly dry bread.

A large, work-roughened finger and thumb gently tipped up her chin but still she wouldn't look at him.

'Your lashes are damp,' was his damning verdict.

'Must be the humidity.'

She heard him chuckle and flicked her misty eyes up in surprise. Her stomach turned over and she forgot her sorrow. He looked absolutely drop-dead gorgeous when he laughed, his white teeth good enough for a toothpaste ad.

'The air is dry,' he reminded her.

'All right. I was thinking of something sad,' she amended sheepishly. And, to divert his intense and unnerving interest, she said, 'My parents died here.'

His hand released her chin, the shadows beneath his strong cheekbones deeper now.

'Is that why you left for England?' he asked tightly.

'My grandpa fled from Portugal with me in tow,' she admitted.

There was a long silence. 'Tough,' he said eventually.

Maddy shrugged. 'We managed, between us.'

'Different climate, culture—and you grieving—' he began.

'When you have things to do, day by day, hour by hour,' she broke in hastily, not wanting to remember her immense loneliness and sense of loss, 'it helps you to get through difficulties.'

There was an expression resembling grudging admiration in his eyes. 'And yet the memories have upset you.'

'Only for a moment. I'm fine now,' she said firmly. 'I— I hadn't realised that coming here would bring it all back so forcefully.'

'Life's hell enough as it is without actively encouraging sad thoughts,' he muttered.

Maddy felt an overwhelming sense of melancholy on his behalf.

'Tell me what's so awful about your life and I'll see what I can do,' she said earnestly, leaning forward in her eagerness to help.

When he frowned and narrowed his eyes speculatively at her, she realised she'd made a big mistake. The new, revised Maddy wouldn't show her emotions. She wouldn't have a tender heart, either.

Worryingly, her carefully constructed façade was crumbling away and she was revealing the caring person beneath. She was jeopardising her chance of success before she even met Dexter.

Some extrovert behaviour was needed rather urgently. And just as she was beginning to panic beneath the driver's puzzled gaze, someone rescued her by striking up a tune on a tinny piano.

Delighted, she breathed a sigh of relief. Yes. That would do. Not the cancan perhaps, but something like it. She bestowed a creamy smile on the driver and sought to allay his suspicions that she might be a tart with a heart.

'You look surprised. But I enjoy the power I get from twisting men round my little finger,' she murmured, inventing rapidly. 'So you tell me what you want and I'll work on Dexter till you get it. Think about it. In the meantime, 'scuse me. Girl's gotta dance.'

And she leapt to her feet, calling for a salsa, indicating with her body what she wanted. The pianist came close to the right rhythm, near enough for her to display a talent that even she didn't know she had. But she'd watched enough TV to know how it was done and thought she managed very well.

So did the villagers. Soon she was being whirled around from man to man and was thoroughly enjoying herself. Every now and then she caught a glimpse of the truck driver, who wasn't amused at all.

Suddenly he rose, knocked back the last of his brandy and inhaled sharply as the raw alcohol hit his throat and shot through his system like a rocket. But he was perfectly sober, she could see that, his eyes hard and clear, his body rock-solid in its aggressive stance.

He jerked his head. It was the age-old chauvinist's interpretation of Shall we go? and just one step up from a caveman grabbing his woman's hair and dragging her off. In true macho style and without caring whether she followed or not, he made his ill-tempered exit.

Breathless and bright-eyed from dancing, she ran out after him.

'Wait!' she gasped, afraid he'd leave her behind. When he turned, his angry expression almost crushed her, till she remembered who she was and stood up to him. 'I was having fun!' she complained.

'Do it in your own time,' he growled, and climbed into the cab.

She had no option but to follow.

'Spoilsport,' she grumbled, playing her role to the full.

He looked furious.

'There are more important things in life than having fun,' he snapped in disgust.

Once she would have agreed. Now she knew that fun was part of life. Without a sprinkling of laughter and enjoyment, the world could be a dark and dreary place.

In the short time she'd been prancing about in her eye-catching get-up, she'd seen loads of people smiling—sometimes at her, sometimes with her. It didn't matter. Only that for a while she'd been surrounded by happy faces instead of gloomy ones.

But it wasn't any use telling the morose driver that. He was having troubles that he didn't want to share. She brightened. She'd make enquiries. Find out what his problem was, and see if she could help.

There was silence between them from that moment on and for a while she dozed. When she woke, she saw from

the signs that they'd passed the town of Luz and were turning onto a minor road which she didn't recognise.

Maddy frowned. 'This isn't the way to the Quinta,' she
declared suspiciously.

'No.'

Her eyes flashed with anger. Strong and silent was OK,
but sometimes it got on your nerves.

'So where are you taking me?' she asked, with enough
steel in her query to tell him that she wasn't going to be
messed about.

'Hotel Caterina.'

She quailed. 'I can't afford a hotel!' she squeaked in
alarm.

'You're that poor?' He shot her an interested glance.

'Don't let the glitter fool you,' she sighed. 'Beneath the
glitzy appearance lies a poverty-stricken woman with
barely enough to get by.' Her voice was shaking with anx-
iety. The little money she had was precious and hard-
earned—and there wasn't any more where it had come
from. Her eyes became pleading. 'Please, take me to the
Quinta, where the accommodation's free.'

'Mrs Fitzgerald's paying,' he told her gruffly. 'You're
staying at the hotel tonight and going on to the farm in the
morning.' A pair of dark, stone-hard eyes met her puzzled
gaze. 'Mrs Fitzgerald is also staying at the hotel.'

It seemed an odd thing to do, when the farm was a few
miles away.

'Why?'

He frowned, as if puzzled by her question.

'It's the best one around,' he replied, making Maddy
none the wiser. 'She's giving a dinner party tonight.' His
lip curled. 'That's why you're in the hotel. You're the guest
of honour.'

Maddy groaned before she remembered she was a party girl and would love such occasions.

'I haven't anything to wear,' she invented hastily and, remembering her role, she tried widening her eyes appealingly, adding a wicked, 'Mind you, I have this saucy spangly affair with a marabou trim...'

She wilted beneath the contemptuous stare.

'A little too much for the Algarve, I think. You'll do very well dressed as you are,' he drawled, pulling into a drive lined with palm trees and oleander.

'You don't like me, do you? Why?' she asked, revelling in the freedom of her unconventional bluntness.

'I'm not particularly interested in you one way or the other. But if pushed, I'd say you are too obvious,' was the cool reply.

He had taste, at least, she thought with amusement. And then her eyes brightened at the sight of the elegant hotel in its carefully manicured gardens. She beamed. A night here would be the height of luxury—and she hadn't had any of that in the last twenty years.

He drew the truck to a halt, leapt out and unloaded her luggage. Then, seeing she'd scrambled down and was stretching her stiff limbs, he clambered back into the cab and drove away, abandoning her—and her luggage—on the driveway!

Astounded, she stood there, open-mouthed and muttering rude things under her breath, then irritably hauled her case to the entrance. The man had no manners. If ever they met up again, she'd get her own back, she promised angrily. *With compound interest.*

Alongside a gang of men, Dexter worked at the ruined Quinta, sifting and sorting till his muscles screamed. Now they'd cleared most of the collapsed timbers and stone he hoped to find family documents and salvageable treasures. Something of his mother's would be a bonus. Just one thing to remember her by. All he had was the dog-eared photograph in his wallet.

The light faded. They worked by arc lamps and then it was time to pack up. Depressed by his lack of success, he stumbled into his car and headed for the hotel, where he picked up his room key and spent a relaxing hour in the bath.

Luxuriating in the deep suds, he tried to imagine his grandmother's face when she came face to face with Maddy. He smiled to himself, wishing he could have been there. But then if he had Maddy would have learnt who he really was, and he wanted to surprise her tonight. And then he'd make her life hell.

Slowly he soaped his shoulders, his mind full of her. It seemed inconceivable that the chubby little girl with straggly blonde plaits could have turned into such an up-front woman. Poor Grandmama! Maddy's appearance would appall her!

He suspected that his grandmother had agreed to promote Maddy for his bride because the little girl had always been so meek and malleable.

His grim mouth softened again into a faint smile. Grandmama now knew different! She'd be horrified to think that she had to spend three weeks entertaining the feisty little temptress. That would teach his grandmother to select brides for him!

Dexter surprised himself with a low chuckle. Just thinking about Maddy had energised his tired body.

Grateful for the diversion from the nightmare of the ruined Quinta, he stepped out of the tub to dry himself before wandering into the suite of rooms to gather his clothes together.

Halfway through buttoning his fine linen shirt, he stopped, arrested by a tempting idea. He could pretend to be dazzled by Maddy. In fact, he could show every sign of eagerness for the match that would link their two families.

Clearly Maddy and her grandfather had set their mercenary hearts on the marriage. Old man Cook had often complained that part of the Fitzgerald fortune was morally his.

Dexter's eyes narrowed in determination. By leading her on and raising her hopes to fever pitch—and then dumping her—he'd teach her a salutary lesson. Maybe she wouldn't mess with men again.

A sardonic curl lifted his upper lip. Who was he kidding? She'd keep trying till she landed some unsuspecting, besotted elderly guy with a healthy bank balance and five years to live.

Surprisingly, the thought of the nubile, laughing Maddy tied to an elderly invalid didn't give him the satisfaction it should. He found the idea of gnarled old hands wandering over her firm young body quite disturbing. It would be a waste of her life. She needed a tough, no-nonsense guy to teach her the true values in life...

Damn it! Why was he wasting valuable time by thinking of Maddy's future? She could make her own bed and lie in it—and probably would. He had his own problems to worry about.

And his grandmother had to recognise that he intended to carve his own path in future—and that she must not interfere. He wasn't going to be blackmailed by anyone, not even an eighty-six-year-old lady.

Over and over again he'd told her he would never marry again. Didn't want the anguish and risk of commitment. Didn't want his wings clipped by a wife who'd expect him to stop roaming the world.

Besides, he wouldn't let any woman risk her life in the

kind of places he frequented in his line of work. Not after what had happened to Luisa.

The pain ripped through him so fiercely that he had to stand perfectly still until it had eased. He had loved Luisa so much. Had been ecstatic when she'd become pregnant. At last, he'd thought, he would have a family; people to love and cherish for the rest of his life.

But his wife and unborn child had been snatched from him, just as his parents had been all those years ago. He had never known such anguish. It had crippled him, had paralysed his mind and turned him into a shambling wreck.

And still it hurt whenever he was unwise enough to think about his gentle, sweet Luisa. Hence the fact that he always blocked out the past and kept it locked away so that no one knew how he felt.

Perhaps he should explain to his grandmother that he'd suffered enough and didn't want to, *couldn't* ever love anyone again. Then she might understand. Yes. He'd tell her tonight, during dinner, if an opportunity presented itself.

Musing on this, he adjusted the collar of his dark suit. The dirty truck driver had become the suave heir to a multi-million-pound business. An unexpected grin of mischief split his face. Maddy would be speechless for once when she saw him!

And he'd enjoy giving the little minx a run for her money. Correction, he thought, the grin widening. No money. She'd go home empty-handed and serve her right.

CHAPTER FOUR

THE dinner-party guests had gathered on the terrace above the hotel's swimming pool. His grandmother's friends were normally reserved and totally humourless, but the loss of the Quinta had cast an even greater restriction on any conversation that might remotely be considered cheerful.

As a result, everyone stood stiff with inhibition. In fact, they looked as if they'd been sucking raw lemons. All, that was, except Maddy.

A bright jewel amid his grandmother's drab and morose gathering, she laughed and gestured, her lively face and colourful clothes a startling contrast to the shocked, stony expressions of the people around her.

She didn't seem to give a damn that they were looking down their noses at her, and from his vantage point, partially concealed by a gigantic *Strelitzia reginae*, he found himself admiring her sublime confidence.

Again, everyone seemed mesmerised. The waiters in the dining room, the diners and the staff in Reception were all clearly talking about her. And smiling. No wonder.

This time she'd whisked her hair up to one side and fastened the chaotic burgundy curls with enormous artificial hibiscus flowers in a searing red. The effect was oddly flattering, showing off her fine bone structure and long neck.

With amused dark eyes sparkling at her sheer verve and vivacity, Dexter assessed the shock factor of her outfit and gave it a ten. One of those basque-corset things in poppy-red. Strapless. Coping—just—with her beautiful breasts.

His grandmother's horrified gaze kept drifting to the

heaped mounds above the tight corset, her eyes popping as Maddy energetically made a point and, in consequence, set her bosoms bouncing.

And on one of those bosoms was a tattoo. No, a transfer. It hadn't been there earlier. He would have noticed. He was too far away to see it clearly, but it looked like a snake. And it writhed in a spectacular manner with the sensual undulations of her breast.

He found himself grinning at her audacity and continued his examination avidly. Her long legs were encased in fish-net stockings, her feet in scarlet sandals that must have added two inches to her height. And the skirt in between was…only *just* in between, hugging her hips and emphasising their slenderness.

Well, Miss Cook, he thought with delicious anticipation. Prepare to meet your downfall. Excitement lit his eyes. He continued to grin because he just couldn't help it when he looked at her.

'Oh, look, Sofia!' she was crying, excitedly peering over the balcony at the pool.

His rigid and sour-faced grandmother winced to be so informally addressed and he stifled a chuckle of delight. Far too many people had been crushed by Sofia's severity. Seeing someone so blithely unafraid of her was something of a novelty.

And it came to him then that as a lively and happy five-year-old Maddy had been slapped by his grandmother and called a stupid, naughty child for spilling her fruit juice on an antique table. So in her *early* childhood Maddy had not been nervous or subdued, he thought with increasing interest.

It hadn't taken long, though, for Maddy's domineering grandfather to turn her into a frightened rabbit. And, of course, Maddy's mother had never shown any interest in her daughter, let alone affection and encouragement. Dexter frowned. Much as he despised Jim Cook, at least the man had showered love on his timid child.

And now here she was, her bounce and confidence miraculously restored. His gaze scanned her lissom body as she leaned precariously over the balcony. And he felt his pulses beginning to thud.

'Sofia!' Maddy called again, a sweet tremor in her voice. 'Do come!'

'What?' barked Sofia, looking as if she'd been heavily starched.

'Down there,' sighed Maddy, oddly gentle-faced. 'What a dear little kiddie!'

Sofia looked. So did everyone else, including Dexter, who shifted to the balcony a few feet from the party and glanced over.

A curly-haired little girl and her father were in the pool, and she was blissfully pouring bucket after bucket of water over her besotted father's balding head.

Dex found himself smiling wistfully through the pang that sliced his heart. That could have been him, with his child. He drew in a sharp breath and hid his anguish.

It was then he saw to his alarm that a faint hope had appeared on Sofia's worried face.

'You like children?' she asked.

He froze. His grandmother would forgive inappropriate dress sense if an heir might be in the offing.

Maddy seemed to blink and recoil, then recover herself.

'Love them!' she replied solemnly. 'But I couldn't eat a whole one!'

Sofia's shocked gasp and his roar of surprised laughter coincided. The guests turned to him as he strode forward and he murmured subdued greetings, aware that Maddy was staring at him in astonishment.

He leant forward and kissed his grandmother on her cool, powdery cheeks and under his breath he offered his apologies for his lateness.

'I understand. You have the Quinta on your mind. But we have our guest from England. Let me introduce you,' began his grandmother stiltedly.

'We've met. I did the Faro run instead of Manuel,' he murmured, swiftly forestalling the naming of names for as long as possible and shaking Maddy's hand in a double handclasp. 'You look wonderful, Maddy!' he enthused.

She looked startled and not entirely pleased.

'I do?' she said doubtfully.

'Stunning,' he assured her, letting his voice take on a gravelly depth.

After a gulp, she fluttered her lashes heavily. She seemed to take a deep breath and then she let her hand wander up his arm to stroke his bicep.

'Rascal! You really know how to get round a girl,' she cooed, making him wonder if that wasn't a Deep South accent that had crept into her flirty declaration. 'My, oh, my!' she declared, even more Scarlett O'Hara than before, widening her eyes and exploring the muscle beneath his soft wool suit more thoroughly. 'How big and strong you are!'

The breathless silence around them was palpable. Any minute now and she'd say Fiddle-de-dee! Struggling between laughter and an odd tight sensation in his chest, Dex turned to his grandmother.

'Don't you think Maddy is refreshingly different?' he murmured.

Sofia Fitzgerald looked very pale and shocked. 'Different, yes,' she agreed as if about to choke on the word.

'I know what you must be thinking. But don't be surprised at my taste in men, Sofia,' confided Maddy, patting his grandmother's shoulder in a breathtakingly condescending way that had everyone present drawing in a gasp of horror. 'I've always gone for the hunky labouring type. Not thin men or intellectual types. Earthy guys can make one feel gloriously feminine, don't you agree?'

Dexter had a hard job keeping his face straight. He was delighted that Maddy was digging her own grave. His grandmother had gone a strange shade of grey.

'I—I think we'll go in to dinner,' she croaked.

'Good.' He grabbed Maddy's hand and threaded her arm through his. 'We'll sit together. Shall we go ahead?'

He was moving away before there could be any demur. The *maître d'* smoothly began to seat the group and Dexter helped, ensuring that his grandmother was placed at the far end of the table.

'I'm amazed,' Maddy whispered, whilst the guests were still milling about and organising their jackets, wraps and handbags. 'I wouldn't have thought that Mrs Fitzgerald would have asked her truck driver to dinner.' She sat down and grinned. 'Though you scrub up well.'

'Thank you. Bread roll?' he offered innocently, pulling his chair close.

'Please.' She slanted him an uncertain look. 'Um... Dexter isn't here yet. When's he coming? I'm *so* eager to meet him.'

To give her a little clue, he shot his cuff, deliberately exposing his all-singing, all-dancing, state-of-the-art platinum watch. Maddy stared at it and he imagined cynically that she must be working out its value.

'What a beautiful watch! How can you afford that?' she cried in amazement.

'Present.' From him to him.

'Ah.' She nodded. 'A woman was involved, I bet.'

He smiled mysteriously, supposing that the female assistant in the jeweller's could be included in that category.

'Wow.' Maddy seemed a little subdued, the smile more uncertain. 'She must be loaded,' she said with a sudden show of confidence. She nudged him and gave him a theatrical wink. 'You're doing all right there.'

It was impossible to prevent an irritated intake of breath. Why was she always going on about money? She was obsessed by it, he thought angrily.

'I've said something to offend you,' she said, her face concerned. 'Sorry. My big mouth. Forgive me,' she mumbled.

He didn't understand her reversal of mood from cynical and sassy to anxious and caring. There was definitely something odd about her manner. He'd noticed before that sometimes she gave the impression of being sensitive—like the old Maddy—beneath that brittle, brash exterior.

Staring into her eyes in an attempt to see past the glittery surface, he found himself caught by her molten grey gaze. And hastily looked away because he felt so unsettled by her. There was something not quite right about her, but he couldn't work out what it was.

'Tell me,' he said, consumed with interest and trying to hide that fact by intently adjusting and readjusting the position of his knife and fork. 'Who is the real Maddy Cook?'

He sensed her body stiffening and he knew he'd hit a nerve. So he risked glancing at her again. She was swallowing. And panic showed in those amazing eyes. She was clearly hunting around for a plausible answer. Fascinating, he thought.

Then she shrugged her beautiful shoulders.

'Someone who realises she's annoyed you,' she said lightly.

'Does that matter?' he murmured.

'Oh, yes!' she avowed, actually sounding sincere.

'I'm flattered,' he said drily.

'Don't be,' she replied with crushing honesty. 'It's just that I don't want to get on the wrong side of you because I think I might need an ally.'

'And why might you need an ally?' he asked smoothly.

'I'm on a mission,' she declared. 'To marry Dex.'

He breathed in and out several times before replying.

'And you think I can help with that?'

'You might. You seem to be a favourite of Sofia's. You could put a good word in for me and tell her how much I want to be his wife,' she finished, sounding pleased with herself. 'Incidentally, you didn't answer my question when I asked where he was.'

Time to reveal himself. He gave a small smile.

'He arrived a while ago.'

The long dark lashes blinked and she cautiously looked around the gloom-ridden table. Since no one else there was under sixty, her gaze soon returned to him.

'Where is he, then?' she asked. 'There isn't even a spare place set for him. I don't understand what you're saying.'

He took her slender hand and gazed into her eyes in simulated desire. Well, OK. Not that simulated.

He stroked his thumb across her palm and she blinked, her lips parting. Oddly, her skin seemed work-worn. Presumably she had to do the chores if the Cooks were poor. Though he couldn't imagine a woman like this scrubbing a kitchen floor. It was another piece of information that didn't fit.

'A small subterfuge,' he murmured as sexily as he could, wondering why he had the urge to draw closer. No matter. It suited his purpose.

He was almost breathing her breath. And finding her

proximity incredibly arousing. He cleared his throat, trying
to keep his head above water.

'I thought you'd be amused,' he husked.

Her gaze was solemn and puzzled.

'I might be, but I haven't got the joke yet—'

'Dexter!' snapped his grandmother sharply. 'You choose
the wine.'

Maddy's grey eyes widened and paled to a soft silver.
She looked so vulnerable suddenly that he found himself
weakening towards her.

'*You?*' she croaked eventually, snatching her hand away
as if he'd savaged it with his teeth. 'You can't be...
Dexter?'

He nodded, telling himself that he ought to be pleased
with her reaction. She was on the make. He had to remember that.

'Good joke, eh?'

'But...' Clearly flustered, she peered deeply into his eyes
and a flicker of fire spurted through his veins. 'Where, then,
are your glasses?' she demanded, tossing her head with a
wonderful defiance.

He had to clear his throat again before answering.

'In a rubbish tip somewhere in Rio, I imagine. My sight's
been corrected by lasers. It means I can gaze deeply into
your eyes and see your soul,' he added, wondering if he
was going a chat up line too far.

Although she gulped—perhaps because his corny line
was too hard to swallow, he thought in amusement—she
didn't look convinced.

'Lasers?' she queried, seeming to pull herself together.
'If you're peering into my soul then they probably im-
planted X-ray machines into your eyes.'

He chuckled. 'Amazing, modern science, isn't it?'

She looked him up and down. Mostly up, because of his height.

'Dex was unusually short. You're tall,' she said suspiciously.

'I grew,' he informed her, solemn-faced. 'Shot up when I was a teenager. Up and out.'

'*That* much?' she cried doubtfully, slowly making a repeat tour of his healthy torso.

With her sultry gaze on his body, the breath came quick and fast from his contracting lungs. Maddy certainly knew how to turn a man on, he thought angrily.

'I worked out. Got tired of being pushed around,' he replied in all truth.

'But you were so skinny!' she declared, glaring from beneath her brows at the breadth of his shoulders. Her pout troubled him but he wasn't sure why.

'I ate like a horse,' he said, having difficulty with his throat again.

She threw him a look of disbelief.

'You were...' she bit her lip and appeared to be considering her words carefully '...kind of cool. Aloof.'

He grinned. 'It was the only way I knew to stay out of trouble—at school and at home. Low profile and all that sort of thing. Head below the parapet. But I'm not cool or aloof now, am I?'

'N-no.'

To his relief, Maddy sat back in her chair and the intense atmosphere seemed to lighten a little.

'That's why I don't think you're Dex at all,' she pronounced scornfully, her beautiful eyes as hard as slate. 'Forget it. It won't work.'

He frowned. 'What do you mean?'

'People don't change that much. You're in league with

Dex. This is some kind of a plot to get me married off to the wrong guy—'

'No plot, I can assure you,' he purred, taking the opportunity to stroke her bare arm. The snake expanded and contracted with her rising breasts and he felt slightly intoxicated. Obviously with triumph. He'd succeeded in rendering Maddy speechless—no mean feat. 'So,' he continued in an intimate whisper, putting a hot hand on her knee. 'Let's get to know one another better. Starting…somewhere around… *here*.'

Maddy jumped and surprised him by blushing before pushing his hand away.

'Dexter!' commanded his grandmother, her voice querulous with fear. 'The wine! And do consult the menu or we'll be here all night.'

'Excuse me. I'll be with you in a moment. Keep the pot boiling,' he murmured to Maddy, and turned to the patient wine waiter.

She didn't believe him. He wasn't Dexter. Not in a million years. It was absolutely impossible. Women could be altered out of all recognition by makeovers, but not men. She seethed with anger at the trick that was being played on her.

Grandfather had been wrong. The Fitzgeralds weren't interested in healing the differences between the two families with a dynastic marriage. They'd responded to his suggestion by actually trying to make a fool out of her!

The hand slipped around her thigh again and gave another little squeeze. Seething with anger, she wanted to stab it with her fork, but summoned up a girly simper instead, when the so-called Dexter glanced back at her.

He stared for a breath-holding second or two and the sultry desire in his eyes made her stomach somersault.

Rage at her own susceptibility scoured her body. However, it wasn't surprising that she fancied him. That had probably been the plan, anyway. Pay a good-looking, impoverished guy the right amount of money and he'd be willing to sell his soul, let alone seduce an innocent English girl. Poor mutt. She pitied him, whoever he was.

But how dared the Fitzgeralds do this to her? It was a vile thing to do! Tightening her muscles as the impostor's hand began to investigate the silky terrain of her bare thigh, she ground her teeth in fury.

She would expose him for the fraud he was. And then she'd demand to see the real Dex. That would unnerve them.

'Hey, ho! This brings back the memories,' she mused sweetly, when the so-called Dexter smiled at her longingly, all soulful eyes and hungry mouth.

His fingers ceased to explore her thigh. He looked shifty, as well he might.

'What does?' he asked cautiously.

'All these people around the table.' Conquering her rocketing pulses, she adopted a dreamy expression, determined to catch him out. 'Reminds me of family dinners around the fireside.'

'We always ate formally, at the table,' he drawled. 'Your memory's faulty.'

She felt a little disappointed. OK. So he'd done a bit of homework. She'd try something else.

'I was young,' she dismissed airily. 'Hard to remember. So much is a blur. I do recall the stone lions on the gateposts—'

'Pineapples,' he said laconically.

'Oh. Well, what about the time your father decorated your bedroom with spaceships and you painted over them with trains—?'

'Trees. Mountains. Poppy fields.'

Dex's father had gone berserk. 'And he loved them,' she persisted.

'He ranted and raved.'

'So he did.'

Sobered by the terrible and tragic mismatch between Dex and his hard and sometimes cruel father, she was even more determined to prove that this hunk of a man was a total impostor.

She knew that Dex had been crushed by his father's uncompromisingly harsh methods of child-rearing. And she'd felt sympathy for him.

But this man who'd been trying to explore her thigh clearly wouldn't know fear if it leaped into his truck and changed gear for him.

She fumed. Did he and Sofia think she was blind, or something?

With a shake of her head, she sighed and said, 'I've forgotten so much! For instance...what were the names of the dogs we had?'

'Solo, Scratch and Shuffle,' he replied drily, his eyes keen and alert as if he knew exactly what she was doing. 'You chose their names, I recall, to fit their characters.'

Maddy racked her brains for something only the real Dexter would know and came up with something deeply personal. Consequently her tender heart made her hesitate before using it as proof. She could be treading on delicate ground here. But nothing ventured, nothing gained. She had to know the truth.

'Dear little things,' she cooed. 'They were a comfort to us both—'

'Yes,' he broke in thoughtfully. 'You often rushed off to cuddle one of them when your grandfather shouted at you for some minor misdemeanour.'

She blinked, disconcerted. But anyone could have known that.

'And there was that day when you returned from boarding-school in England with a black eye,' she said lightly, 'and Scratch jumped up in welcome and you sat down and buried your face in his furry ruff—'

'Shuffle,' he said curtly, cutting her off. 'And it was a broken nose—'

'Oh, yes. How did you get that?' she asked, assuming a concerned expression.

'You know very well,' he drawled cynically.

'Perhaps I do, perhaps I don't,' she said equably. She did her big-eyes routine at him. 'But if you're Dexter you'll be able to jog my memory. And you'll be able to confirm how old you were at the time.'

'Why should I?' he growled.

Was he stalling because he didn't know? Her eyes met his in challenge and she faltered, almost gasping at the Arctic frost of his expression.

'You—you want to prove who you are, don't you? The right answer would convince me,' she stumbled.

She felt sick, knowing that only Dex would have found the memory uncomfortable. A truck driver would neither know nor care. If this *was* Dex, by some miracle, then she would regret upsetting him with unpleasant memories.

Aghast at what she'd done, she bit her lip, wishing she hadn't strayed into such personal territory.

On Dexter's return to Portugal for the summer holiday, a farm hand had been sent to collect him from the airport because the whole family—bar Maddy herself—had gone to a villa-promotions exhibition in Lisbon.

So it had been she who'd gently asked what had happened and who had damaged his face.

And, although he'd been his usual stoic, contained self,

she'd recognised how deeply hurt he'd been. He didn't care about his physical injuries, only that the girl he'd adored from afar had rejected him.

Oblivious of the diners around them, they let their gazes lock. And she saw that he was hurt—and furious, too. It *was* him! she thought, aghast.

'OK. If it'll satisfy you,' he snarled.

She winced. 'No. Don't bother. You—you…don't have to—'

'Too late. I think I do.' His eyes glittered, his voice harsh and grating. She cringed. 'I was nearly fourteen. I'd chatted up someone else's girlfriend at the end-of-term dance and I was dragged outside and thoroughly beaten up. My time at boarding-school was hell on earth, and only you and I know about it because I always put my bruises down to boisterous rugby games. Now do you believe who I am?' he finished with quiet vehemence.

She wished the earth would swallow her up. Oh, yes. This *was* Dexter! No longer a browbeaten, bullied teenager, but the kind of charismatic sex-god who'd never be turned down by any sane woman with a healthy libido.

Incredible. Judging by his performance so far, he could play the caveman and urban sophisticate equally well. Those eyes hinted that he could be a tiger in bed. She was already sexually aroused by him and he hadn't even touched her.

Help. Her intention was to flirt outrageously with him— and turn him against her! Was she mad, or what? The man was bad and dangerous to know. She was an innocent, straying into an alien territory where Dexter roamed with confidence.

If she spent too long with him she could see herself wilting beneath his overpowering sex appeal and she'd find herself between the sheets with him, minus her virginity.

Just another woman who'd succumbed to Dex's almost hypnotic masculinity.

Could she really keep him at arm's length whilst appearing to lead him on? Could she keep herself from letting him know that she longed to be kissed into willing submission by that fascinating, sensually curving mouth?

Panic welled up inside her. She was in terrible trouble! The next few days were going to be a dreadful ordeal!

CHAPTER FIVE

MADDY summoned up all her strength of will and put together a bright smile with a lot of teeth showing.

'Yes,' she breathed, secretly daunted by the task she'd set herself. 'I do accept it's you, Dex.' Her eyes pleaded with him. 'Sorry I brought up the past.'

His eyes flickered. 'Apology accepted.'

'Good.'

The Dexter she'd known had certainly vanished. This one was sexually aware and sure of himself. No one would kick sand in his face. But he'd lost his tender heart on the way.

She trembled, wondering if he took after his arrogant, ruthless father—or his mother, who she'd initially remembered as kind and gentle. Until her grandfather had put her right and told her that the woman had been a tramp.

He smiled a little sardonically at her confused expression.

'Shall we start again?' he suggested.

She managed a smile. 'Why not?'

'Well, hello, then,' he murmured, leaning forward and kissing her cheek.

The unexpected warmth of his lips, the prolonged—it was, wasn't it? For it certainly seemed to last forever—lingering pressure conspired to send her senses into free fall. And she felt more scared than ever.

'Hello!' she gasped stupidly as he drew away a fraction, his face remaining breathtakingly close.

'Friends again, I hope. It's going to be a pleasure to renew our acquaintance,' he said silkily.

'Er—yes. Lovely,' she quavered, struggling with an impulse to haul him back for a proper kiss.

Her mouth was tingling with hunger and she was shocked by the wicked urges which seemed intent on overriding common sense and decency.

He stared deep into her cleavage.

'Whereabouts shall we start?' he breathed in heartflipping gravelly tones.

Her tinkling laugh sounded hollow and slightly hysterical.

'You know, I can't get over you!' she declared throatily, avoiding an answer that might encourage him. 'You're so...amazingly different—'

'So are you.'

The languorous and velvety tones were so warm and intimate that she almost confessed. But flashed a broad smile instead.

'I re-made myself,' she said, injecting a note of pride into her voice.

'With dramatic results,' he murmured, taking her hand.

His wink and accompanying leer worried her but she managed a coy giggle of self-deprecation.

'More flattery, please!' she purred. 'And while you're at it you can satisfy my curiosity. You're trotting out the compliments now, and yet you were curt and rude to me when we first met. So what's changed?' she asked innocently.

He gave her the benefit of his dazzling smile and pool-dark eyes.

'Let's be frank. Our grandparents have hopes of marriage between us, yes?'

'So I was led to believe,' she hedged.

'OK. To be honest, initially I didn't like the idea of being pushed into marriage with someone I'd remembered as drab with the personality of a limp cucumber,' he told her with brutal frankness.

'Thanks.'

A cucumber! Rot him. He was right, she thought wryly. And she grinned to show there was no ill feeling.

His eyes danced. And more. There was…admiration? Certainly desire. In buckets. She felt her body quiver.

'My pleasure,' he said with a chuckle, nibbling her knuckles.

'So?' Stupid though it was, the feel of his mouth was robbing her of speech. Or perhaps it was the lowered flutter of his impossibly thick black lashes. And his gently savaging teeth, promising… Maddy hastily pulled herself together and searched for the question she'd meant to ask. 'So,' she said, appalled at how croaky she sounded. 'What changed your mind?'

'You did.'

He was croaky too. Maddy began to panic. Dex wasn't supposed to be attracted to her!

'I did?' she squeaked in alarm.

'Very much so,' he murmured. 'You are…' his slow gaze burned all the way from the top of her head to her feet, stopping at strategic points in between '…a knock-out,' he said on a husky out-breath.

She swallowed, her smoky eyes enormous with dismay.

'Oh. I thought you might find me…not to your liking!'

'I was startled when I first saw you,' he admitted. 'And I was bearing a grudge on behalf of my family.'

'Why?' she asked, startled.

'Because your father seduced my mother.'

She blinked. 'The other way round, surely!'

'I think you'll find I'm right,' he drawled. 'In any case, you grew on me. It took a while for me to take on board the fact that you'd gone through a transformation, and that maybe we could...' His eyes kindled, lighting instant fires inside her. 'Er—how shall I put this delicately?—maybe we could get together. Close together. You're fascinating, Maddy,' he said passionately. 'I'm intrigued. And very, very attracted.'

She gulped again. Help again! Now what? He couldn't possibly see her as his bride, so he must be interested in her as a 'good-time girl'. There were enough hints in his sultry eyes for even the most unsophisticated woman to interpret correctly. No doubt he thought that she was such a fun-loving modern woman she'd be willing to go to bed with him!

It was a nightmare situation that she'd created. She could hardly go back to being dull again.

This called for drastic measures. She'd raise her game. Become so eager for a ring on her finger that he'd run a mile.

And so she leaned towards him, her eyelids working overtime.

'They tell me you're a multimillionaire,' she breathed, hoping her expression looked greedy enough.

And she was sure he winced before the megawatt charm was turned back on. After all, she reasoned, no man wanted to have his wallet admired more than himself.

'Can't deny that,' he said with a sickly smile.

'Good. I adore rich men. My sort of guys.' She drew in a steadying breath and daringly forced herself to say, 'Couldn't lend me fifty quid, could you?'

This time, to her delight, he gulped visibly. But he reached inside his jacket again and peeled off several escudo notes. She took her time counting them and did a rough calculation, deliberately using her fingers and moving her lips to appear stupid. Approximately one hundred pounds!

'That do?' he enquired.

Conscious that the whole table was watching them in stunned silence, Maddy eagerly took the notes, held them up to the light in what she hoped was an expert way, then stuffed them into her cleavage, wondering how far he'd go in his attempts to lure her into his bed.

'Nicely, thanks—for the moment. I adore a generous man,' she husked, giving him the full Mata Hari come-on. And more loudly she added, 'What can I do for you in return?'

A glass crashed to the floor at the other end of the table. Maddy saw Mrs Fitzgerald struggling with her blood pressure while a waiter replaced the champagne flute she'd smashed and beckoned for reinforcements to clear the broken glass on the tiled floor.

'I have a very long list of suggestions,' Dexter said quietly, and she found herself trembling at what those might be, the warmth in her loins pooling as her imagination ran riot.

'And for you, madam?' murmured the *maître d'* close by Maddy, his pen poised, notebook in hand.

A bucket of water and lots of ice, she almost replied in panic. No. Make that two: one for Dex, one for herself.

She looked up, glad of the diversion from Dex's hot, mesmeric eyes. The *maître d'* was having difficulty controlling his mouth. He dearly wanted to laugh. She pulled herself together hastily.

'I'll have orange sweet-potato soup with chilli and coriander, then sole with samphire and girolles—and could you do a side-dish of chips with that and a bottle of brown sauce, please?' she asked loudly, disconcerted by Dexter's smothered chuckle.

'Certainly, madam,' the man said, still desperately trying to keep a straight face.

'You're a doll,' she told him, affectionately patting his arm. And whispered, 'Go on. Laugh. You know you want to.'

He grinned and she laughed with him, glad of a crack in the funereal atmosphere. Then, greatly daring, she jumped to her feet and declared to the mute and miserable guests, 'A toast!' Politely but warily they raised their champagne glasses. Sofia looked daggers at her. She beamed. 'To marriage!' she cried. And when the glasses were hovering uncertainly in mid-air she added recklessly, 'May the rich always marry the poor and even things out.'

No one moved. But Dexter was laughing and drained his flute with enthusiasm.

'You're fantastic,' he cried in genuine amusement, much to her disappointment. 'Utterly unique. Where have you been all my life?'

Damn, she thought. 'Clapham,' she answered.

And tried to engage the man on her left in conversation. However, the dullness of his responses flattened her mood, and it wasn't until her soup had come and she was wickedly slurping it with noisy appreciation that her spirits lifted again, perhaps aided by the arrival of an electronic-keyboard player who'd begun to fill the dining room with a medley of old favourites.

No one clapped when he finished, so she did—vigorously. And from then on a few other diners—none in the Fitzgerald party, though—gave the hard-working musician a desultory clap too.

Frantic to be declared unsuitable as a bride and to be thrown out, she racked her brains for something to seal her fate.

The rest of the guests at her table sat in morose silence

and would have crushed the most determined optimist, but she cheered herself up with her pièce de résistance, picking up the soup bowl and drinking the final dregs from it.

'Waste not, want not,' she declared chirpily.

And judging by the cold stare from Sofia she'd succeeded in killing any lingering thoughts of marriage.

Relieved beyond measure, she beamed at everyone, seeing herself packing her bags in a few days, once she'd established the terrible events following her father's disappearance.

Very satisfactory, she thought smugly. The lecherous Dexter could find himself both a mistress and a bride from other sources.

It was then that she realised how odd it was that a man as wildly eligible as Dexter was still single. Of course, it hadn't been surprising when she'd believed that he was an older version of the emotionally restrained boy she'd once known.

But now she'd met the new and charismatic Dex his single status didn't make sense. By all rights he ought to have been snaffled up ages ago, by a willowy beauty with an aristocratic background and a taste for lusty men.

Being outspoken had its advantages. She was able to ask.

'Dex, do you have hidden flaws I don't know about?'

He quirked an amused eyebrow at her.

'Only the kind you'd enjoy.'

Her throat dried at his wicked expression but she kept her bright smile going.

'I meant,' she said reprovingly, giving him a playful push and feeling way, way out of her depth, 'the kind of flaws that would explain why you're not already married.'

She thought his mouth thinned, but then he put his arm around her chair and leant close to whisper intimately in her ear.

'Perhaps I've been waiting for the right woman. Someone with hair the colour of rhubarb wine, the directness of a Roman road and a way with social niceties that would make a Neanderthal blink.'

Was he mocking her? He'd said all that with intense passion, as if he adored her unconventional behaviour. And yet his choice of words wasn't exactly flattering. Whatever he'd intended, she'd call his bluff.

'You say the nicest things,' she preened, patting his smooth, warm cheek and marvelling at the flurries of pleasure that such a simple action had aroused in her. He smelt gorgeous. Felt even better.

'The things I *do* are even nicer,' he breathed huskily.

From any other man that comment would have been corny and worthy of a laugh. Not the way Dex had said it and not the way he'd looked at her. Hot. Steaming. Bone-meltingly sensual.

Hardly able to think straight, Maddy did a bit of eyelash fluttering and hastily tore off a chunk of roll and chewed it, wondering how she could stop Dexter blowing on her ear because it was causing mayhem throughout her body.

Fortunately, clearly worried about the danger Maddy posed to her precious grandson, Sofia called out imperiously from the end of the table.

'Tell me, Maddy. Do you work?'

Overjoyed at the diversion, she made a face. 'I did. I'm unemployed now. I think women are meant to be supported by men, don't you?'

Pinch-mouthed, Sofia shot Dexter warning glances, but he stroked Maddy's arm as if mesmerised and wouldn't mind a parasitic wife at all.

And now she felt an unwelcome tingle spreading deliciously along her veins. Heavens. The loathsome man was dynamite!

'Don't you have any ambition?' persisted Sofia sternly.

Maddy adopted a look of wide-eyed innocence. 'Other than to be rich?'

'Other,' agreed Sofia in choking tones, 'than to be rich.'

Maddy tried to concentrate. It wasn't easy and took all her will-power, because she really wanted to grab Dexter and let him kiss her stupid.

But she was stupid *enough*, she mused with a rueful smile. Otherwise she would never have been attracted to such a smoothie as Dexter Fitzgerald.

'I thought about being a lap dancer,' she replied honestly, having discussed the occupation with her friends—though in a tone of astonishment that anyone could find the nerve to do such a thing.

'A...lap dancer!' cried Sofia in undisguised horror.

Maddy took a deep breath, knowing she had to be as unappealing as possible.

'Fabulous wages, lovely sparkly clothes, loads of admirers—what more could a girl want?' she enthused evasively, thinking, A heck of a lot more!

'She'd be good,' Dexter avowed with earnest enthusiasm. 'You should see her move! Maddy,' he urged, his black eyes wickedly taunting as they dared her, 'why don't you cheer everyone up and show them the true extent of your talents?'

For a moment she was nonplussed, and then realised this would be a perfect opportunity. After her display Sofia Fitzgerald would disinherit Dexter if he continued to show interest in her!

She beamed in relief, wondering why she hadn't thought of that. It would, in addition, get her away from Dexter's overpowering presence for a while.

'I will,' she purred seductively. 'Hold on to your hats, folks.'

And, grabbing the nearest waiter, she tottered onto the small area in front of the musician, gleefully aware that the Fitzgerald guests—including Sofia—had been struck dumb by her choice of partner.

To her delight she discovered that the waiter was a great dancer. She began to relive the happiness she'd felt in her early teens, partnering her grandfather at the business functions they'd attended when he was struggling to attract investors.

The hotel guests began to smile and clap and one or two couples came onto the restricted square of floor to join them. Because of her evident joy, the atmosphere in the dining room had changed from a whispering stuffiness to one of laughing chatter. She'd broken the ice. And she realised she was having a fantastic time.

This was true freedom, something she'd never known. Not being subjected to her grandfather's increasingly petty commands. Not listening to his bitter complaints about the injustices he'd suffered. Not being browbeaten into wearing unattractive clothes, and not, absolutely not, biting her tongue if she disagreed with his pronouncements.

As she dipped and swayed and laughed for sheer delight, her body strangely supple and responsive to the music, she knew she'd never be the same again. She felt strong. A woman reborn.

The dance ended, the waiter reluctantly excused himself and the *maître d'* took his place as a rock tune began. Happy beyond belief at her liberation, she let out a whoop and enthusiastically gave herself to the fast, exhilarating rhythm till the notes died away and she stood breathless and pink from exertion, glowing from the storm of applause.

Until she was swept into stronger arms and pressed, chest to knee, to a harder, hotter body.

Dexter, her senses told her before she even glanced at his dark, sensual face.

She gasped, overwhelmed by sensations that crowded her brain and body with illicit thoughts. Dreamy music flooded her ears. Dexter's now familiar scent of clean masculinity filled her nostrils.

The pure angle of his tanned, satin-touch jaw and smiling mouth transfixed her eyes, and the feel of him, the sheer authority of his powerful body, wrecked her former sense of being in control.

He breathed into her ear again. His clasp was possessive and commanding. The languid, smoochy melody lured her muscles into liquid compliance as the two of them moved as one person in an effortless response to the slow, haunting beat.

She seemed to be melting in his arms. And he was hard and hungry against her, leaving her in no doubt as to the extent of his lust.

Bemused, she tried to speak, but found herself gazing into his eyes and drowning instead, her entire body lique-fying and seeming to flow into his. Their heat mingled and flames began to lick through every vein she possessed.

'Maddy! You're everything I ever dreamed of! What a bride you'll make!'

'A—a bride?' she stammered, hastily revising her opinion that he only had lust on his mind.

'I can see it now,' he rhapsodised. 'Lace. The rustle of taffeta. And you could wear something nice, too—'

'You're kidding me!' she said crossly, highly suspicious of his sense of humour and terrified that he was responding so positively to her shocking behaviour.

'I'm thinking of our wedding night now…oh, Maddy,' he groaned. 'I can't stand being so close to you and going no further! Shall we slip away? I can show you my flaws, one by one,' he murmured, nibbling her sensitised ear.

Yes, oh, yes! was her knee-jerk response. Fortunately her mouth was slower.

'We couldn't! It would be rude,' she stumbled out thickly.

'To look at my flaws?'

'To leave!'

He laughed. 'That sounds an unusually prim remark. I'm surprised you give a damn. You seem singularly unconventional to me.'

Maddy could have kicked herself. He was right. A heartless tramp wouldn't have good manners.

'I thought it would bother *you* if we vanished,' she amended hastily. 'I'm sure you don't want to upset your grandmother.'

He ignored her excuse. 'Look at this! Your snake transfer has smudged,' he whispered, the tip of his forefinger tracing its outline.

She couldn't breathe. With a huge effort of will she drew back, on the pretence of checking.

'I must get that permanently tattooed,' she husked out.

'It occurred to me that you're such a modern woman I would have thought you'd have your navel pierced,' he mused, his fingers surreptitiously investigating her abdomen with insolent thoroughness. His head lifted and his eyes met hers with lazy amusement. 'Unless you've gone in for body adornment somewhere else?'

It was a moment before she could speak.

'That's for me to know and you to wonder,' she countered archly.

'Perhaps,' he purred, his breath making the hairs on her neck stand to attention, 'you could take me on a mystery tour of the places of interest.' And Maddy knew he wasn't talking about tourist sites. 'You know, I'm looking forward to being with you over the next few weeks—'

'I doubt I'll stay that long,' she replied, managing to sound regretful. 'I don't think your grandmother is convinced of my suitability as a future wife for you.'

'What's she got to do with it? It's not my grandmama you have to convince,' he whispered. 'You must realise what you're doing to me, Maddy.'

Maddy stared at him wide-eyed, horrified by the shocking, wilful urges that tempted her to encourange Dexter. The strong hand on her hip, the fingers sifting gently through her hair and the husky voice telling her in breath-shortening detail what he intended to do with her once they were alone, told her that Dexter had been well and truly hooked.

Everything had gone wrong! She'd wanted to frighten him away! And her numb and stupid brain was too busy with the exciting images conjured up by his hoarse, sexy suggestions to focus on a way out of her dilemma.

'...Touching you, every inch, kissing the line of your hipbone, inhaling the warmth of your—'

'Please!' she whispered faintly.

'I have every intention of doing so, as soon as we can escape,' he assured her. 'I assume you prefer action to advance information?' he muttered thickly.

Her huge eyes met his and she was both aroused and unnerved by the returning blaze of passion. She wanted him to kiss her, more than anything in the world. Her body swayed and he held her tightly, his mouth inches from her upturned face.

Hopeless! It was all going haywire, she thought helplessly. Horribly, messily *wrong*.

CHAPTER SIX

HER eyes closed. And in a flash she had her answer. Almost weeping with relief, she managed a sigh, patted his cheek with a shaking hand and said with genuine regret, 'Down, tiger. It's out of the question.'

His response was a low, tigerish growl of desire. Breathing hard, she managed to make a gap open up between them by pushing against his chest. Her fingers toyed flirtatiously with the top of his open shirt until she accidentally felt the fierce beat of his pulse at his throat.

Feeling desperately light-headed at the erratic leaping beneath her fingers, she tried to remember what she'd intended to say. Get a grip, Maddy, she told herself sharply. Don't weaken. And she removed her fingers from the temptation of his warm, satiny skin.

'Why is it out of the question?' he breathed.

In the subdued light of the now crowded floor, he ensured his broad, obscuring back was to Sofia's table before capturing her fingers in his. He brought them to his mouth and kissed them. Then he gently sucked her forefinger, his gaze hotly intent on hers.

Corny again. Horribly effective, though. She could barely think, let alone speak coherently.

'Grandfather,' she husked shakily. And decided to be honest. 'You're driving me crazy, Dexter,' she admitted, allowing her lips to assume a pout. 'But he'd never forgive me if I didn't get a ring on my finger before I let you beyond first base.'

She was released. His expression was unreadable.

'Marriage first, sex after?' he asked in strangled tones.

She'd got him. He didn't want marriage at all and her insistence on it was putting him off.

'That's about it. A girl has to look after her interests,' she ventured, trembling like a leaf.

His jaw suddenly looked as solid as granite and she knew that he was annoyed. A man thwarted in sex was potentially dangerous.

'Determined little minx, aren't you?' he murmured with a half-smile, but his eyes were veiled with steely lights.

Maddy suppressed a shudder of apprehension. But she'd got herself off the hook.

'Hungry, actually. I'm ready for my chips,' she announced brightly, wondering how on earth she could force a morsel down her. 'They've been keeping them hot for me, I think.'

'Put me on the back burner if you want,' he drawled as he walked her back to her chair. 'But since you lit me up, I reckon it's up to you to damp down my flames.'

'I suggest a swim if you're hot,' she said, without really thinking.

His salacious grin had her stomach swooping with peculiar twinges. 'What a good idea,' he murmured. 'Meet you by the pool at midnight.'

Appalled, she gave a little nod. And decided to publicise their tryst to foil him. Sofia would join them if she thought any hanky-panky was on the menu.

'We're going for a midnight swim,' she announced chirpily to everyone at the table. 'Anyone else coming?'

Sofia put down her fork with a clatter. 'Dexter,' she said sharply, 'you need your sleep. I expressly forbid you to stay up late. The Quinta is more important than anything—'

'Even an heir?' he enquired mildly.

The old lady drew herself up with regal hauteur but her

lip was quivering. Dexter immediately strode to the end of the table and put an arm around his grandmother's shoulders, speaking quietly to her.

After a while he kissed the relieved-looking Sofia on the forehead, bowed to the company and, to Maddy's astonishment, he quietly excused himself.

After that, Maddy felt gloom settle on her. Sofia seemed oddly relaxed, and had begun to loosen up with her friends. Now that Dex had gone the tension had gone too, but so had the adrenaline buzz that his presence had aroused in her.

With nothing better to do, she ate her meal, ignored by the guests, and declined the pudding. Pleading tiredness, she trudged wearily up to her room and rang her grandfather, reporting quite honestly that things had gone well.

She had decided that she would let him down gently, tell him face to face that the marriage bid had been unsuccessful.

Feeling very flat, she got ready for bed, thinking that Dexter wasn't going to be easy to manage at all. His response to her flirting had been totally unexpected. So had her own reaction to him.

Somehow she had to continue to be the most unsuitable bride this side of Frankenstein's laboratory. She had to act as if she was desperate to get married, whilst keeping the over-eager Dexter at bay.

The situation was complicated by the fact that he was devastatingly sexy. As a consequence, she found herself wanting him—even though she knew perfectly well that he was only interested in her body and didn't care about her at all.

The change in him was amazing. Who would have thought he'd become such a cynical, lecherous Casanova?

Brushing her hair in front of the mirror, she stared at her

plain, unadorned face and wished she didn't have to act the trollop any more.

Though…she would never go back to being a doormat again. Not now she'd tasted independence. The new Maddy was OTT, but some things she'd done had been fun, and the characterisation had changed her forever.

The things the new Maddy said had come from somewhere inside her. She had more power to think for herself than she'd realised.

When she returned home, she mused, amazed by the unusual sparkle in her eyes and the animation of her features, she'd strike a happy medium.

Not too selfish, not too self-effacing.

'Dexter,' she said happily, 'you've done me a favour. I can be gorgeous. I can have a personality.'

She hugged herself with glee and scrambled into bed. An entirely new Maddy would be born: one she liked, one she could respect. And, as a result, she felt in her bones that she'd find peace of mind and happiness at last.

He was waiting for her in the foyer the next morning, dressed in truck-driver mode. The black T-shirt was clean and figure-hugging, the jeans freshly laundered too. And just looking at him made her knees go weak.

Fortunately she'd dressed to kill. Or, rather, to give herself courage and to remind herself of the kind of person she was supposed to be. A woman of the world. Not a naïve idiot who melted every time a handsome man gazed at her.

So, to go with her spiky pony-tail, which she'd encircled with streams of pink ribbons, Maddy had opted for pink wedge sandals, cut-off denim shorts embroidered with sequins and a luminous yellow top.

The outfit had made the waiters smile at breakfast and the service at her table had been more than attentive.

Dexter's reaction was more visceral, his strangled intake of breath causing her heart to thump frantically with unwanted excitement.

'Hi,' she said, sounding more eager and breathy than she'd intended.

'Hi,' he drawled, in a slow, liquid tone that accompanied his equally slow and liquid trawl of her body.

'I'm ready,' she said into the silence, wondering why her lungs had collapsed without warning.

'So was I, last night. I waited by the pool. You didn't come,' he accused, his eyes doing their best to strip her naked where she stood.

She waited till the annoying quivers had died down before replying, by pretending to be bothered by the tangled tassels on her waist-cinching belt.

'Let me.'

And before she could stop him Dexter had stepped forwards, his fingers untwisting the tassels. Her stomach sucked in of its own accord as she tried to avoid the tantalising touch of his fingers.

They were beautiful, she thought hazily. Long, slender, strong and neatly manicured. They also were intrusive, and she realised after a while that he was deliberately brushing her smooth skin and letting his fingers linger more than strictly necessary.

Struggling for control, she grabbed his hands and pushed them away.

'Hands off the goods! You deserved to be stood up after pretending to be a mere employee, instead of lovely, wealthy Dexter, heir to the Fitzgerald millions,' she pouted.

'You're so frank,' he said, his voice reverberating huskily. 'Still, at least I know where I stand.'

Maddy tried a gold-digging smirk.

'You'll get a lot for your money.'

His admiring glance roamed freely over her body.

'That's true.'

She frowned as he picked up her case and indicated that she should follow. How could she find him so incredibly attractive when she despised him?

'You left rather abruptly last night,' she remarked, unable to hide the disappointment.

Her resentment appalled her. Despite all the dangers in the situation, she'd wanted him to dance with her all night and to flirt with her. It had been so boring when he'd gone.

'I had to.'

His hand attached itself to the small of her back, fitting perfectly in the gap between the hem of her cropped top and the swinging tassels of her belt. She found herself sinking into the warmth of that hand and suddenly repressed an urge to whirl around and press herself against him.

She was shocked. Her behaviour was beginning to mimic that of the moral-free woman she was pretending to be!

'You could have stayed. I thought you were your own man?' she challenged a little shakily.

'I am.' The hand shifted downwards and she could feel her rear being massaged by it as she executed her Monroe wiggle. 'But I knew I'd do something outrageous if I stayed around you any longer. Like...kissing you in the middle of the dance floor. Or running my hands over your body. My grandmother would have been shocked. So I made my excuses and left. Besides, I had a busy day ahead of me. This morning I've already put in a few hours of work, and once I've dropped you off I'll have another eight hours of slaving away.'

'You work hard for a rich man,' she husked, desperately trying to stay in control. 'I wouldn't bother if I had as much money as you.'

Her breathing was definitely in trouble. Fortunately

they'd reached his truck and they'd both stopped. Unfortunately Dexter had turned her to face him and she was beginning to panic.

If he kissed her she'd have to stay cool. React with enjoyment, like a seasoned flirt. And not go all gooey. She wasn't sure she could manage that.

Would he kiss her? A finger was idly tracing her cheek. She dared not look up but kept her gaze fixed intently on his pecs. Which seemed to be heaving about rather a lot. She swallowed.

'Work hard, play hard. I'd hoped to see you at the pool,' he growled. 'To be more private.'

'I got bored and went to bed,' she admitted.

'That's nice to know,' he murmured, his forefinger lightly outlining her mouth. 'But if you'd come as promised I would have relieved your...boredom.'

Her stomach bucked. Any minute now and she'd take his finger in her teeth and slowly nibble it. Shaking, she fought for sanity.

'Naughty!' she trilled, managing to escape. 'You know I'm unavailable until our wedding night. Incidentally, what did you say to your grandmother before you left?' she asked curiously. 'She stopped flinging filthy looks at me. I wondered why.'

His eyes looked slightly mocking.

'I reassured her.'

'About me? That's nice. How?' she demanded, covering up her alarm.

Her heart thudded. Sofia's opposition was central to her plan! How could he have made a wacky bride-to-be from hell seem acceptable?

He smiled. 'I told her I'd fallen for you in a big way. And I pointed out that you had child-bearing hips.'

Maddy felt a dagger spearing her chest and turned her

reaction into a cough. The hips might be right, but her womb wasn't, she thought miserably. Still she had to live with that and not feel sorry for herself. However hard that might be.

'They're not that big,' she said tightly.

His hand explored them. 'No. Just rounded enough,' he whispered intimately.

'So…she was pleased with what she saw?' she asked in private dismay.

Dexter placed her case carefully in the truck and held out his hand to help her up, giving her a pat on the rear as she clambered in. He leaned his brawny arms on the seat where she'd settled herself, his pose confiding.

The heat of his flesh spread into her naked thigh and it was all she could do not to move away in panic. Or kiss his upturned face. She stared at him, appalled by everything that was happening.

'She'll come round,' he offered. 'I'm all she has now. In the long run, she'll go along with whatever I want.' His voice became husky and he stroked her thigh idly. 'And she knows I have designs on you.'

'Oh!' Maddy felt a spurt of dread. Or was it something else, caused by the hypnotic rhythm of Dexter's wicked fingers? 'She…she wasn't alarmed by my appearance, or anything?' she squeaked. 'People sometimes are.'

He considered this solemnly. 'Surprised. You're like nothing we've ever seen before,' he admitted. 'But when I spoke to her she realised that her opinion was unimportant. And we could always work on your clothes sense and table manners when we're married,' he added condescendingly. 'I'm the one who'll be climbing into bed with you, not her.' His eyes kindled. 'And that's where the action'll be, where my heir will be conceived.'

Maddy couldn't speak. She'd never provide anyone with

a child. Why did he keep talking about it? Over and over again he kept stabbing her in the heart with the cruel reality.

Seeing he was expecting some kind of response, she nodded vigorously, and he seemed satisfied because he gave a quiet smile to himself, patted her thigh and gave it a squeeze, then walked around the truck to haul himself up into the driver's seat.

The vehicle roared into life and they set off.

'Thinking of us in bed?' he murmured.

'What do you think?' she whispered hoarsely.

And then she did visualise them together. It wasn't the nightmare scenario it should have been. More a blissful entwining of his tanned limbs with hers, the feel of his firm body, masterful and insistent...

She groaned, despairing at her susceptibility. But then she was inexperienced and Dexter knew exactly which buttons to push to raise the temperature.

Some serious gold-digging was needed or she'd be reaching two hundred degrees centigrade and melting into his arms.

'Marriage,' she mused dreamily, with only a hint of a croak. 'So it's really happening! I can't wait. All that lovely money. I'll shop till I drop. Just let me get my hands on that plastic! Will I get an allowance, Dex? And Grandpa will need a new home and a full-time nurse. I suppose his treatment will cost a lot, but you can afford it.' She clasped her hands in what she hoped looked like ecstasy. 'We can have loads of holidays,' she gloated. 'Cruises, in the best cabin suites. Visits to London and New York, Paris, Hong Kong—'

'Any other reason why you want to marry me?' he asked drily as he swung off the road and headed for the foothills of the Monchique mountain range.

She let herself ponder on this for a moment.

'No, I don't think so. It's strictly a business arrangement isn't it? You get my body and I get your loot.'

He laughed. Threw back his head and roared.

'What did I say?' she cried, mesmerised by the texture of his golden throat.

'You're priceless,' he chuckled.

'No. I've got a price. It's marriage,' she retorted cheerily, thinking of the shock his ego would get when he realised she had no intention of going anywhere near a three tiered cake, bridesmaids or a groom.

'You want that very much, don't you?'

'A rich man's bride,' she sighed ecstatically. 'What girl wouldn't?'

She looked away from his amused face. It was worrying that she loved it when he laughed. That was when he was at his most dangerous. So she concentrated on the scenery.

'What girl? One who was a romantic and believed in true love,' he suggested drily.

With some difficulty, she ensured that her hand dismissed such an idea as hopeless.

'Romantics end up poor. Love can't buy nice clothes,' she said earnestly.

'No,' he said, his tone quiet and faintly disappointed.

'It can't even buy lovely scenery,' she said, genuinely entranced by the views. 'If you're rich you can choose somewhere fabulous to live, like the Quinta.'

'You like what you see?' he asked in a low voice.

Her eyes found his and her heart did its familiar somersault. Yes, she liked what she saw. But, mindful of the sexual threat he posed, she fixed her gaze dreamily on the landscape.

'Very much,' she said, her love of the inland scenery softening her voice and making her eyes shine with pleasure. 'I do. There's been such a lot of new building and newly constructed roads that I thought the countryside might have vanished beneath acres of concrete. But it's still here and just as beautiful.'

'Have you missed it?' he enquired.

'I've been so busy I've hardly had time to think of my life here,' she said, her voice a mere whisper. But, yes, she missed it. She missed her beloved father desperately. Wished she felt the same about her mother, but then she'd hardly ever seen her. She'd always been shopping or staying in Lisbon, with her friends.

But she'd missed the warm climate. The freedom to run around the spacious Quinta or the acres and acres of meadow and woodland...

She pulled herself sternly together. It was no good moping over the past. Anyway, she had plans that would improve her future considerably.

Dexter asked no more questions, his face set in serious lines as if he, too, was lost in reverie.

After a while, Maddy was able to relax and enjoy the drive, though it seemed to her that Dex had taken them on a roundabout route—perhaps to avoid the main road. He'd always adored the countryside too.

Away from the coast and its—admittedly pretty—clusters of white villas, geraniums, palm trees and bougainvillaea, the landscape was very different. Lusher, more gentle.

Here there were fields with roaming Landrace pigs, and sturdy horses nuzzling the buttercups. Little Roman bridges arched languidly over silvery rivers and old men paused in tending flocks of goats to watch the truck go slowly by, answering Dex's wave with cheery greetings.

The soil, she knew, was deep black and fertile, fed by the network of streams that trickled down from the high Serra de Monchique. She screwed her eyes up. On some of the poorer soils of the hills she could make out the white flowers of the scrub cistus and the small beige shapes of Churro sheep, grazing contentedly.

Here and there were cork oak and eucalyptus plantations. The oak was a rich dark green, many of the trees pruned for charcoal and also to form a wide flat canopy that would shade domestic animals. In contrast, the tall eucalyptus looked misty blue and merged with the mysterious haze of the distant mountains.

A calmness quietened her senses. For as long as she could remember she'd been living on the edge. Initially when she'd arrived in England she'd tried to be all things to her grandfather: confidante, helper, housekeeper and sounding-box. Later her duties had extended to those of provider and carer.

She'd never really had a childhood after the age of eleven, or a teenage life, either. And money worries had filled her mind day after day.

And now there was this latest stress; the need to foil the plot to marry her off—whilst preventing her grandfather from risking apoplexy at being thwarted.

She sighed. In addition to that, there was now Dexter's determined campaign to seduce her.

It seemed to Maddy that the pressure had been immense for years and years. Yet today she was smiling, discovering for once what it was like to feel totally at ease. In these surroundings she could keep a sense of balance. She had forgotten how beautiful it was and how much she knew of the land and its flora and fauna.

There had been good times here when she'd escaped her strict, widowed grandpa. She and her adored father had walked companionably together. With loving joy he had introduced her to the plants and flowers of the region and taught her to identify the birds by their song and their flight.

She'd even enjoyed one or two happy picnics with Dex,

when the two of them had slipped from the house, away from the tensions which were mounting between the two families.

Delighted to be back, she wound down the window and let the breeze caress her face. The entrancingly evocative perfume of the scented oils from the maquis scrub tantalised her nostrils and she sighed with deep pleasure.

'The journey's taking longer than I imagined,' she said drowsily, her head lifted to bask in the sun's rays. 'Not that I mind. It's heavenly.'

Nevertheless, she gradually began to take a more alert note of her surroundings, hoping to see the entrance to the Quinta estate any moment.

After a while, she sensed that something wasn't right. It occurred to her that she knew the shape of that mountain far ahead, and they ought to be further to the east of it.

And now Dexter was turning onto a narrow, bumpy track that she didn't recognise at all. Her body grew tense, that lovely sense of comfort evaporating. He was up to something.

'This isn't the Quinta road,' she said sharply.

He looked scathing, as if she'd said something stupid. 'Of course it isn't!'

The lurching truck clattered over a series of potholes, temporarily robbing her of breath. She hung on to her boob tube as a precaution, conscious of Dexter's frequent sideways glances. Either he'd come this way to test the strength of Lycra, or he was taking her somewhere private. She trembled, afraid that she'd roused something in him that was beyond her ability to handle.

'So where are we going?' she asked with remarkable calmness.

'The pigsty, of course.'

'The pigsty. Yes, what else?' she said, as if talking to an imbecile.

It had been on the extreme western edge of the estate, far from the farmhouse. A series of low hills had separated the pig-house and its surrounding meadows from the main bulk of the Fitzgerald land. She could see the hills now, their gentle bulk hiding the Quinta and its rolling acres from sight.

In the far distance she could identify the small white dot that must be the pigsty. As far as she could remember it had been nothing more than four stone walls and a corrugated-iron roof with concrete bays.

At least, she consoled herself, he couldn't be planning a seduction in a place of his choice. Pig muck and sex didn't exactly go together.

'Would you like to elaborate?' she asked sweetly.

'Not much to say. It'll be rather cramped and basic, but I'm sure you won't mind,' he imparted.

Startled, she stared at the isolated stone building. 'I won't mind...what?' she asked, a terrible suspicion forming in her mind.

'Staying there.' The truck shuddered over another collection of huge potholes.

'Me?' she squeaked. 'Stay in that little chunk of stones with a tin roof?'

'It's been done up as an emergency home,' he defended solemnly. 'Almost habitable.'

Maddy took a deep breath. 'Tell me this is another of your jokes! Dexter! Stop fooling about—'

'No fooling,' he assured her, frowning. 'We agreed it would be the best solution. It's clean and dry. There's a stove, and we've put glass in the windows and tiles on the roof.'

'Fascinating. My compliments to the glazier. But I didn't

agree to anything. I'm staying at the Quinta,' she told him firmly.

'Don't be silly—' he growled.

'Don't you silly me!' she flared. 'How dare you stick me in a pigsty? You have at least eight bedrooms in the farmhouse and I don't see why— What are you doing, trying to kill me?' she yelled as the truck screeched to a stop.

He looked at her, astonished. 'I don't believe it!'

'What? What don't you believe?' she demanded.

Then he smiled. The smile became a chuckle and turned into a laugh. During which he revved up the truck and hurtled towards the pigsty.

'Oh, Maddy!' he roared, shaking his head, vastly amused.

'Answer me!' she insisted. 'What's so funny?'

'It doesn't matter,' he said, trying to control his laughter. His twinkling eyes danced merrily at her. 'But I think you've been made a fool of.'

'How? Why? Who by?' she demanded.

'Your grandfather.'

'*How?*' she yelled.

'He knew you were coming here and didn't tell you.'

'Tell me what?'

'You'll find out,' he said callously. 'Here we are, Maddy. Home sweet home. With my compliments.'

Boiling with fury, she folded her arms in mutiny as he drew up beside the small building. Wisely taking the precaution of removing the keys this time, he jumped out, collected her luggage, then hauled open her door with a familiar screech of metal.

'I don't see any telephone wires,' she said suddenly.

'That's because there aren't any.'

Her eyes widened. 'But I have people to ring! Grandpa, and the rugby team—'

'You can borrow my mobile. Just say the word,' he drawled.

'I won't need to. Because I'm not getting out,' she muttered grimly.

'I think you will.' His eyes sparkled with mischief. 'Even if I have to lift you out myself.'

'You and whose army?'

'Me and my biceps. Hurry up. I must get to work.'

She glared. He and his biceps could easily manhandle her. And she didn't want to be crushed against his chest or to find herself helpless in his arms. Who knew where that might lead? A real fear swept over her and she flew to her own defence with a vengeance.

'Don't you dare touch me!' she yelled.

'Go on,' he goaded. 'Let me wrestle you out of there. We'd both enjoy it.'

'Not when I'm mad at you!' she stormed.

'Those fabulous eyes,' he murmured. 'They're crackling with anger. You really turn me on, Maddy.'

Alarm bells sounded. She recognised the danger signs. They were in an isolated spot and he thought she was game for anything. Time she cooled him down.

'I thought I was going to be pampered,' she muttered sulkily. 'Live in luxury. What is this, some kind of test?'

'Why don't you come down and find out? Or would you like me to grab you—'

'No!' she cried hastily, and scrambled out. She tried to think of a reason and was amazed how fast she came up with one. 'You'd ruin my outfit and I'd break my nails! OK. I'm down now. So tell me why I'm to be stuck out here instead of knocking back champagne and oysters,' she demanded, putting on a haughty expression.

'It's for your own good,' he soothed. 'You wanted somewhere cheap, this is it.'

Forgetting her role, she flung her head up, her eyes blazing with anger and humiliation.

'Is that what you told your grandmother last night? Is that why she seemed to be placated? It was your idea, wasn't it? You said you'd dump me in the pigsty and she was thrilled, wasn't she?'

'I can assure you that you were put here for your convenience,' he murmured.

'Con*ven*ience?' she protested.

'It was arranged some time ago. Our grandparents thought it was an excellent solution.'

'I fail to see why!'

'Privacy,' he said, his expression managing to be both sexy and amused. 'Intimacy.'

'Uhh... For...you and me?' she asked, with a hasty gulp.

'That's right,' he purred. 'Somewhere we could be alone. Our grandparents wanted to throw us together and the cottage is ideal as it's miles from anywhere. And, of course, you have no transport. The perfect lovers' hide-away, don't you think?'

Somehow she kept her cool. He wouldn't dare to touch her against her wishes. And he had kept on insisting that he was anxious to leave for work so that didn't give him much time to pounce.

If he turned up later, hoping for someone to soothe his aching muscles with a sensual pre-engagement massage, she could barricade the door and keep him out.

She quivered, the scene that had flashed through her mind far too vivid for comfort. Dexter, stripped to the waist and sitting at her feet. She, expertly easing the knots and tensions in his back. He'd turn. Pull her onto his lap with a fluid movement and...

Nervously she licked her lips, banishing the Technicolor consequences with ruthless haste.

'I don't have much choice, do I?' she said throatily.

He grinned. 'None at all.'

Trying not to let her conflicting feelings show, she muttered, 'Just remember you'll get nothing from me till I have what I want. If you thought that you could keep me here so the isolation would wear me down and I'd be putty in your hands and I'd do anything to get into a decent bed and clean sheets, even if it meant sharing those with you, then…'

She paused. Took a deep breath. Whilst she'd been talking Maddy had been thinking rapidly. The silence, the placid beauty of her surroundings had deeply penetrated her mind. She could hear warblers and cirl buntings, and there were speckled wood and hairstreak butterflies flirting with the carpet of wild flowers in the nearby meadow.

The landscape drew her. Its better memories haunted her mind with their tantalising moments of happiness. For a short time she longed to relive those joyful times she'd shared with her father.

And after a while she would insist on knowing exactly what had happened that cold October day when she and Dexter had become orphans. Then she'd go home. Wiser and more independent than before.

Maybe the false Maddy would have squealed with horror at being here, and demanded wall-to-wall diamanté panelling and a Jacuzzi or two. But she was fed up with maintaining this act and wanted time to be herself.

She met his gloating smile with her level gaze. Even now she could see that he thought he could persuade her to take the easy way out, to opt for the luxury of the Quinta and his waiting arms instead of this simple little cottage.

He meant to dangle the prospect of luxury and comfort in front of her eyes and expected her to agree to anything he proposed. Well, he was wrong. She'd love it here.

'Then?' he prompted, looking justifiably wary.

'Dex,' she said, her tone warm with contentment, 'I'm not alarmed at all.' She began to march towards the plank door and flung over her shoulder, 'In fact, I'm delighted. Bring my gear, will you?'

It would be wonderful, she thought, deeply happy. A holiday. The first she'd had since she was a kiddie. Time to think and breathe, space to walk and wander, an opportunity to take stock of her life.

Thanks, Dexter, she thought once more. This time, the joke's on you.

CHAPTER SEVEN

HIS frame filled the doorway, blocking out the light. 'Your luggage,' he said, his tone totally without expression. And he moved forwards, allowing the sunlight to stream into the small room.

Giving him a brief nod of thanks, she looked around with pleasure. It was basic, but the apartment she shared with her grandfather wasn't much better.

At least this was cosy, with a fireplace for the cool evenings, comfortable armchairs and a sofa, a table, and a wood-burning range in the surprisingly modern kitchen all in the same room.

She stretched languidly, revelling in the prospect of solitude. He'd be gone soon and she'd be left alone. Fantastic.

'There's no electricity and no hot water yet,' he pointed out.

What did she care? The freedom overcame all discomfort.

'There's a kettle. I can boil water in it on the stove. And I can swim in the river.'

He moved closer, dominating the room, his eyes dark and thoughtful.

'Difficult to wash clothes.'

She laughed. 'You are so wicked, Dex! If you think you can lure me to the Quinta by waggling the joys of a washing machine at me then you're mistaken! I'll rough it if I have to. I have a far greater prize in mind. You!'

Teasingly she poked his chest. Scowling, he grabbed her

wrist and pulled her angrily against him, his arm encircling her body and holding her prisoner.

Determined not to let him have any power over her, she fought the wave of pleasure that it gave her to be in his arms.

'I thought you'd be horrified,' he growled, clearly perplexed.

She'd ruined his plan! Her eyes twinkled.

'I bet!' Her lips parted over pearly teeth and she laughed at his dismay. 'Don't let this flibbertigibbet exterior fool you, Dex,' she cried merrily. 'You won't dissuade me. I know the outcome I want.' A release from this stupid marriage idea, she thought. Information. Then a hasty retreat back to England. She beamed. 'The stakes are high. And I'm tougher than you think.'

'We'll see,' he murmured, his dark eyes kindling.

In an instant, Maddy felt her elation dying away. He had cupped her face in his hands, forcing her to look at him. His mouth looked hungry. She felt a shaft of fear and excitement scythe through her body and she gave a small gasp as it burrowed hot and hard into her loins.

'Work to do,' she reminded him breathlessly.

'Yes.'

Deliberately, Dexter angled his head, his black lashes a sweet crescent on his tanned cheekbones. And she couldn't move because she wanted his kiss so much, had often imagined that firm, sultry mouth descending on hers and taking savage possession.

'Maddy,' he breathed.

Her eyes closed. Dreamily she lifted her face to his as his hands slipped away to force her so hard against his body that she could feel...everything.

This was dangerous. Stupid, some part of her brain told her. And she ignored the warning. Sank contentedly into him. Placed her arms around his neck and stroked his glossy hair.

There was the lightest brush of warmth against her lips and she gave a low moan. Then suddenly she was being pushed backwards until she could feel her spine against a wooden door.

Her eyes opened, huge, grey and startled. He was looking at her in confusion but when her now drowsy gaze met his, he gave a sharp exclamation and finally, wonderfully, seared her lips with his.

She felt soft and yielding. Her mouth opened, pliant beneath his, her moans enticing him on. He hadn't meant to do this. Had intended to dump her in the cottage and tell her in triumph that she hadn't a cat's chance in hell of marrying him. Then he'd planned to pick her up four days later and...

Her mouth. Warm. Moist. Driving him wild. The most perfect body writhing against him. A scent of something fleeting...like the sweet fragrance of choisya. He couldn't get enough of her. Hands, fingers, arms, legs, body, wrapping around, touching, crushing, invading...

A deeper groan. His. The sweet rise of her breasts against his fevered lips. The arch of her body, encouraging him to greater intimacy. Shaking like a leaf, he let his trembling fingers wander across the gleaming mounds above the buttercup-yellow top. He licked his lips, hardly able to breathe. And then came to his senses.

He had to get out of this unscathed. She'd got under his skin. Amused him. Annoyed him. Aroused his admiration and his long-lost sense of fun in equal parts, and had insinuated herself into his mind and non-existent sex-life until he didn't know whether he was coming or going.

Wryly he acknowledged that it would have to be the latter.

'Time flies,' he husked.

She stiffened and the spell was broken. Driving mockery into his eyes, he stepped back, almost overcome by the vulnerable and bewildered expression on her flushed face.

But he could see it was an act. She'd known exactly what she was doing. Her sex appeal was her only weapon and she had no compunctions about using it to land herself a rich husband.

Her chin lifted and the defiance of her gaze confirmed his suspicions. So did her offhand dismissal of their passionate encounter.

'You'd better be off, then.'

'See you.'

He gave her a casual wave and heaved his leaden limbs into motion, not trusting himself to stop till he reached the truck.

For a moment he hung onto the wheel arch, fighting for normality. And then, angry with himself for being seduced by a cheap little tramp with her wares on display for all to see, he stormed into the cab and took off at a lick.

Glancing into the side-mirror, he saw the cottage growing smaller and smaller in the distance until it was a tiny blob of white amid the acres of fields.

Whatever she said, he thought with a dark scowl, she'd find it tough and lonely there. Particularly at night.

The pretence of courting her had to stop. He dared not whisper in her ear or stroke her soft skin any longer. It was doing terrible things to his chosen life of celibacy.

If he worked till he dropped and then went to see her he'd be too tired to be aroused. And he'd tell her that evening that now his grandmother had seen the cheap and tarty kind of woman Maddy had become she could forget any idea of marriage.

After that he'd have great pleasure in letting her know

that he'd been stringing her along all the time, to teach her a lesson. His mouth formed into a grim smile. That would be very satisfying!

His mobile trilled. The diggers and bulldozers had arrived. Sternly he put Maddy to the back of his mind and supervised the simultaneous digging of the trenches for new wind-breaks for the proposed plants, the wholesale clearing of the fire-blackened site—apart from the Quinta itself—and the marking-out of foundations for the new offices.

In a few days the site would be levelled and new topsoil delivered. Then he'd have to abandon the search for mementoes in the ruins of the house and order that to be levelled too.

The men worked through the evening with the aid of arc lamps and their own headlights. A hearty mutton stew was delivered but he ate nothing, too busy to spare the time.

Work finished at ten and he joined the men in the temporary open-air showers they'd set up, enjoying their hearty laughter and envying the contentment on their faces as they proudly exchanged news of their wives and families.

But he'd chosen loneliness in preference to being hurt again. When he got his life back he'd be fine. It was just here, with all the memories, that he hankered for something more, something to fill the yawning hole in his heart.

Dexter hated self-pity. He was doing fine. The sooner he got the Quinta up and running and he could get away from all these memories, the better it would be.

Blanking out his destructive thoughts, he eased his weary limbs into the truck, his ears still ringing from the droning noise of the diggers and with the smell of smoke and charred wood lingering in his nostrils.

As he crested the hill dividing the cottage from the Quinta, he saw that a welcoming light burned in the cottage and a thin spiral of smoke was rising from the chimney.

His heart lifted with pleasure, almost as if he was coming home.

Though that was ridiculous, and he knew that in actual fact he was only looking forward to crashing into bed.

On a sudden cautionary impulse, he parked at the end of the track and walked the rest in the dark with the aid of a torch. It was a clear night, the stars bright in the dense night canopy, and here the air seemed cool and pure in contrast to the stench around the farm.

There was a surprising spring in his step and he covered the distance in no time. Not long now, he thought, and he'd be fast asleep...

He tensed. It wasn't sleep, but something else that was enticing him. He scowled, shaken by the power of his physical needs. He'd thought he was better than this!

Two choices proposed themselves. He could ignore Maddy—though with some difficulty—or indulge his shocking fantasies to the full.

The prospect of making love to her startled him with its intensity. His heart had leapt and a wild excitement had shot through his body, bringing it to tingling life.

And he knew that he was kidding himself if he thought he could keep his hands off her. His body was screaming for her. For the first time ever, he felt as if his life was hurtling dangerously out of control.

She deserved to be used, he told himself. And a second later he winced with disgust at his lack of principles. Maddy's fault. She'd teased and tormented him till he hardly knew what the devil he was doing, he thought angrily.

Reaching the open window, he paused. She was singing. Incongruously, it was the hymn 'All Things Bright and Beautiful'.

A frown drew his dark brows together. His mouth assumed a sardonic sneer. Surely the thoroughly modern Maddy ought to be belting out a raunchy Madonna melody? This was too sweet, too innocent for a streetwise woman.

She reached the chorus. A shiver went down his back at the pure notes soaring joyfully through the window and disappearing into the hushed night. Clearly she was happy. Contemplating her wealthy marriage, he imagined sourly.

Cautiously he peered in. Something extraordinary had happened. The place was unrecognisable. Tidy. Sparkling. The furniture rearranged.

Ridiculously, he held his breath. She had her back to him and was washing up. An aroma of herbs and spices filled the cottage and he could hear the crackle of a fire in the grate, relieving the coolness of the autumn night. The homeliness of it made his head spin.

And she was the centre of it all. A curvy, sexy female who electrified him from head to foot.

Yet her dress was simple. Pastel-blue cotton, with a collar, sleeves and a hem modestly reaching to mid-calf. When she turned, wiping her hands on a small towel, he drew back into the shadows, but could still see her as she sang her way to the cooking range and put the towel to dry on its rickety rail.

No make-up, he thought, his heart pounding. His head buzzed with confused messages. She was beautiful. Smiling blissfully as though being stranded in the middle of nowhere with the minimum of comforts was entirely to her liking.

Why? *Why?* Had she been playing the part of a sassy siren in order to land a rich husband? Was he seeing the real Maddy now? Or had she merely changed tack?

He thought about this. Certainly he'd made his sexual attraction obvious. She would feel vulnerable with them both sleeping in the cottage. Maybe she was taking steps to protect herself.

He considered this theory, trying to see things from her point of view. Her goal was to keep him at arm's length until her wedding night. Since she'd succeeded in getting him interested, was she now abandoning her seduction and turning herself into an untouchable innocent?

His fists clenched. He wouldn't put it past those damn self-help books to have thought of that one. The author of *Getting Your Man* probably knew all about the male hunger for whores in the bedroom and chaste virgins elsewhere.

Maddy had learnt all the dark arts of allure and was putting them into practical use. He'd probably find a chapter titled *Stoke up the Boilers*, where they advised all would-be brides to withhold their favours and behave like demure Stepford Wives if they wanted to be irresistible.

Cynicism raked the hard planes of his face. She'd find there was a chapter missing in her book. The author had omitted to deal with the problem of men who loathed being manipulated.

Dammit, the woman obsessed him! Was she siren or angel? He intended to find out. To establish once and for all what kind of person she really was.

Gritting his teeth, he strode to the door and wrenched at the handle. Locked. The singing stopped abruptly in mid verse.

'Maddy!' he commanded angrily in the sudden silence. 'Let me in!'

'Dexter! I couldn't! Grandfather wouldn't like it!' she called in defiance, from behind the door.

He muttered a curt oath in Portuguese. 'Open up! I *live* here!' he bellowed in fury.

'Wha-a-at?'

He ground his teeth together. 'Stop playing games! You

must have seen my bedroom! I told you the cottage was for both of us! Let me in. I've had a long day and I'm bushed.'

'I haven't even unpacked, let alone looked at bedrooms!' she yelled. 'I've been so busy... I assumed you meant you'd visit... Oh, Dex, you can't come in! Go to the hotel. You can afford it.'

His scowl would have stripped paint off the door if there'd been any. 'You're a liar, Maddy,' he muttered under his breath. 'You knew I'd be back. And it's time you got your comeuppance.'

Silently he slipped around to the window, leaping in before she remembered it had been open.

When he landed lightly on the floor, her reaction horrified him. Huge-eyed and plainly scared, she spun around and then flattened herself against the door.

'Please!' she begged in terror. 'Don't...don't hurt me—'

'It's me. Dex,' he bit angrily. 'Not a serial rapist on the prowl.'

'But...' She swallowed, trembling with nerves. 'The way you came leaping in, so angry and...' Her voice died away in a croak.

'I told you. I live here and I'm not going to be kept out by anyone, least of all you,' he muttered.

Dexter dumped the bag with his grubby clothes on the floor. His eyes were hard as stone when he said coldly,

'I'm shattered and in no mood for fooling around. This is where I'm crashing out tonight.'

'Oh, help!' she whispered.

Disconcerted by the heaving of her breasts beneath the demure bodice of her dress, he moved towards the kitchen area. She jumped nervously, her hand going to her mouth in alarm.

So vulnerable. So beautiful. Fires roared through his

body, drying his throat and thickening his tongue. In her simple shirtwaister, barefoot and with a scrubbed face, she looked more desirable than his hormones could handle.

'I'm after something to eat, not sex,' he growled, getting the half-lie out with difficulty.

'Oh. Sorry. I—I panicked. I forgot you had a mistress.'

'What?' he asked with an irritable frown. What was she talking about?

'The watch. Your rich woman-friend gave it to you,' she reminded him nervously.

'I don't know why I gave you that impression,' he muttered. 'I bought it myself. I was referring to the female shop assistant when I implied a woman was involved and I wish I hadn't tried to act the man-about-town because it's just not me!'

He found a couple of rolls and some cheese, slammed them on a plate and stumped crossly to the table.

'No...mistress?'

'No woman in my life. Not in that sense,' he grumped. 'Now, if you don't mind, I'm shattered after a hard day. Stop giving me the Inquisition.'

'You...you've been working all this time?' she asked uncertainly, the tension in her body easing a little. When he nodded, suddenly weary, and his shoulders slumped as he contemplated the cheese without interest, she moved from the door and briskly strode to the larder. 'In that case,' she said to his surprise, 'you'll want a proper meal. When did you last eat?'

He furrowed his brow. And wondered cynically if she was doing the 'angel in the kitchen' bit. Chapter ten, perhaps?

'The men made some mutton stew,' he drawled. 'We had that and some sausages and rolls at lunchtime.'

'Nothing since?' Her eyes were dove-soft, wide and concerned. To his rage, he felt his knees weakening at the very sight of her. 'You must be starving.' She turned her back. He was tempted to shape his palms around its curves. 'There's some steak here. I'll put it on the griddle. And do some sauté potatoes,' she said softly. 'How about that?'

He blinked, his mind moving sluggishly. Tiredness or sex on the brain. He wasn't sure. Didn't care, providing he could feast his eyes.

'Yeah. Thanks.' He cleared his throat, dazzled by her as she tucked a tea towel into her belt and bustled about by the sink. The book was working a treat, he thought with a wry smile. 'You didn't want me around a minute ago and now you're Delia Smith. How come?' he remarked huskily, trying to trap her into a confession.

Her breath sucked in. He noticed that her hand shook as she peeled the potatoes.

'I'm being practical. You got in. It would take several hefty men to eject you and I can't lay my hands on any at the moment. So I might as well feed you.' She shot him a quick glance over her shoulder. 'You look shattered. Anyway, woman's got to look after her man, hasn't she?' she finished lightly.

As he'd thought. No real concern. Just a ruthless interpretation of that damn book.

'So what else are you doing for me?' he asked in a mocking tone.

'Peaches,' she said, with a look that meant she knew what he'd been suggesting. 'I picked some earlier.'

He grunted. Peach picking. Very domestic. OK. He'd give her full rein. She clearly had an agenda here to show herself in a favourable light, so he'd listen to it all and let her think he was impressed. Demolishing her hopes afterwards would be even more satisfying.

'What else did you do today?'

He could see she was smiling vaguely and staring into space. The knife which had been deftly slicing the potatoes remained poised in mid-air.

'I explored,' she said softly, her voice warm and liquid with pleasure.

'Tell me. Play Let's Pretend,' he drawled, finding his own tones oddly husky. 'I've come home after a hard day's work and you're going to tell me about your day while I unwind.'

She seemed to tremble, though she could have been stifling a laugh, amused by the ease with which she was able to twist him around her little finger. And, boy, was his stomach in knots.

'OK. If you like. Let's see… When you left, I dumped my stuff and changed into something more suitable for wandering around,' she said quietly, the perfect little obedient wife, entertaining her husband.

'Barefoot, like you are now?' he asked, reluctantly fascinated by the smallness of her feet, the tiny pink toes, the high arch that he could imagine kissing…

'No,' she husked, as if his thoughts were miraculously being transmitted to her mind.

He had to admit that the atmosphere had thickened. There was an electricity in the air, an almost tangible undercurrent swirling into his subconscious and attacking his will-power.

Must be the subdued light of the oil lanterns. Gave a kind of falsely romantic glow—particularly to the delicate planes of Maddy's face.

'I—I had some trainers!' she stammered. 'And an old shirt and jeans—'

'So why aren't you wearing them now?' he asked.

He was a fool. His eyes grew cold and sardonic. He knew

the answer. Because a pastel-blue dress was more feminine. More virginal.

'I got muddy!' she husked.

An image of them both, sliding around in mud together, flicked into his mind and had to be ruthlessly dismissed. Tiredness was making him fantasise. He'd be OK once he'd got some sleep.

'How?' he asked, pretending to sound bored and uninterested.

'I was investigating the reeds by the river and slipped,' she explained with a wry smile. 'I had to boil loads of kettles and saucepans before I could get my clothes clean enough and hang them on the line outside. Anyway,' she went on hastily, 'I found the larder was well stocked, so I stuffed a *paposeco* with salted ham, cheese and salad, and popped some chocolate and bottled water into my shoulder bag. Then I walked up the track as far as the big bridge.'

His eyebrows shot up. 'That's five miles from here!'

'I know. Hang on.'

He was. By his fingertips. With her pink tongue appealingly protruding from her lips in deep concentration, she slid the potatoes into the buttered pan then beat the steak flat and coaxed it onto the griddle. Her tongue slipped back. Dexter let out the breath he'd been holding.

'I didn't realise how far I'd gone. I was too busy enjoying the scenery and remembering,' she said softly.

He felt his stomach tighten.

'Remembering what?'

She leant against the sink, her eyes dreamy.

'Being with my father. Using bamboo poles to shake down pine nuts from the stone pines for pesto. Picking lavender…'

She sniffed at her hands and smiled and he knew that she'd crushed lavender between her slender fingers. With difficulty he resisted the urge to go over to see if he could smell it too.

'I remembered picking figs and almonds, olives and peaches. The tiny yellow narcissi that cover the slopes of the hills. The wonderful cinnamon colour of the cork trees where the bark has been stripped—oh, and the stacks of cork looking like hooped tiles, or curls of chocolate. I remembered the purple oxalis and scilla, the asphodel and orchids in the meadows, the blue jacaranda and the almond blossom in the spring. I listened to the burble of the river and the sound of bees and I was thrilled that I could still identify dozens of different kinds of birds from their song alone. Somewhere in the distance I could hear the drone of machinery, perhaps some new villas being built. And I felt privileged to have this time here, away from all the new developments and far from the concrete of home.'

Her voice died away and she blinked, thinking that she'd strayed too far out of character. Pink-faced, she turned to tend the steak, dismayed that she'd revealed so much of her inner self.

'What then?' was all he said, though he sounded very husky and she wondered if he'd been smoking all day while he worked.

'I wandered back. Scrubbed the kitchen, cleaned the stove, packed it with wood and lit it—and the fire—for a bit of warmth and to dry the place out,' she answered more briskly. 'Then I cooked supper for myself and sat outside looking at the stars. It's a long time since I've seen such a clear night sky. In London the lights are too bright to see the stars properly.' Her expression softened, remembering how they'd twinkled at her as if winking in approval. 'It was so peaceful out there. Time flew by. Then I got a bit chilly and came in to read for a while.'

'Fact or fiction?' he asked, a rather harsh tone to his voice.

'Are you referring to my book, or what I've just told you?'

A small smile. 'The book. Why ever would you lie to me?' he asked with exaggerated innocence.

'Precisely,' she said tartly. 'I was reading fiction. A family saga.'

She pointed to the paperback and he picked it up, glaring at the blurb on the back before discarding it.

'Families!' he muttered in contempt.

And she winced. Yes. Families. Why did she torment herself so?

Dexter got up and pulled a beer from the gas fridge and she was left to cook the meal in silence while he stared moodily at the fire.

She couldn't help but smile wryly. Was this what married life might be like?

'What's so amusing?' he asked, without turning around.

'How did you know I was smiling?' she asked in amazement.

He came to see how she was progressing.

'By your breathing,' he replied unnervingly.

'Oh.' She hoped that he assumed her red face was from the heat of the stove. It was rather disconcerting to think that he'd been so acutely tuned in to her. 'I was thinking about being married,' she said absently.

Dexter grunted. And then she remembered. They'd be spending the night together.

'It's ready. Sit down,' she told him shakily.

'Thank you. Sit with me. We have things to discuss.'

Intrigued, she slid into the chair opposite. At first he toyed with his food and then, after a small mouthful or two, he began to eat with enthusiasm.

'This is good. I didn't know how hungry I was. So. You've enjoyed your day,' he said a little stiltedly.

Her face softened. 'Very much.'

'A change from Clapham.'

Maddy laughed in delight. 'I'll say!'

Without warning, he caught her hand and turned it over, his fingertips feeling the roughness of her skin.

'You do a lot of domestic work,' he observed. 'Is that your job?'

She flushed. 'No. I worked in a children's home until it closed, shortly before I came here.'

Relinquishing his hold on her hand, he leaned back in his chair and studied her carefully.

'A children's home.' His mouth pursed and he speared a piece of potato, conveying it towards his mouth. 'Well, well. Tell me about it,' he murmured drily, almost in challenge. 'What's it like?'

'Not much to tell—'

'Oh, do try. I'm interested,' he said sardonically, as if he didn't believe her at all.

'All right,' she retorted crossly, pulling her hand away and folding her arms in defiance. 'The kids were all sorts. Orphans, delinquents, temporary boarders while their parents or carers were in hospital or jail, children under care orders because they were being abused... We took them all. My job was with the little ones. To give them love and stability and some sense of pride.' She saw his wavering doubts and relaxed her belligerent pose, allowing her passion to show. 'I adored those children, Dex. We had such fun. I'm not ashamed to say that I shed a tear or two when they were bussed off to other homes and the doors were boarded up.'

His eyes had sharpened. A puzzled frown had drawn his dark brows together.

'You cried because you'd lost your job.'

'No, because I knew I'd miss the children desperately,' she corrected, flushing at his sneering insult.

'Hmm.' He wasn't convinced. She'd only generalised. Anyone could have described a home in those terms. 'Caring for children isn't very similar to lap dancing,' he observed cynically.

'Not even close,' she agreed with a small smile.

He tried again to unravel the mystery about her dual personality. 'That doesn't explain the state of your hands.'

She looked ruefully at her work-roughened palms. 'I look after Grandpa. He has exacting standards. Expects the flat to be spotless. That's how I lost weight. From the time we arrived in England, I took on the running of the apartment we moved into while he tried to get a business going.'

Dexter felt shaken. That had the ring of truth about it.

'When you were eleven?' he asked, incredulous. 'You were a kid! What kind of life was that for a child?'

'There's a positive side. It toned my muscles like you wouldn't believe,' she said wryly. 'Some people pay a fortune for a personal trainer. They ought to try lugging shopping about, Hoovering at a run and scrubbing every washable surface to keep fit!' she said with a laugh.

He was stunned, finding it hard to envisage the hard life she'd led. But he knew old man Cook's opinions on how women should be employed. What a vile old man he was.

His eyes darkened to deep jet-black. Knowing Cook as he did, he thought it unlikely that Maddy had been offered any comfort on the death of her parents. And she'd idolised her gentle father. Poor kiddie. He could almost feel sorry for her.

'He shouldn't have turned you into a drudge. You had rights of your own. A child needs to feel secure, to be loved,' he said passionately. Seeing her look of astonishment, he throttled back. 'It must have left you little time for friends,' he said stiffly.

She shrugged. 'Grandpa needed me. I could see that. He was helpless in the house. And he was distraught when his business folded, so I did what I could to keep things running smoothly. But I have friends. I don't see them often, but they're staunch and I can rely on them.'

Dexter thought of the nervous young child he'd known. How she must have mourned her parents—and the lifestyle she'd once enjoyed—when she'd discovered herself in a cramped flat in England instead of roaming around the elegant and spacious Quinta.

It must have been one hell of a shock. He frowned. What of her teenage years? He looked at her and suddenly wanted to know everything about her.

'I suppose things changed once you started work and began dating,' he suggested.

'Hardly!' she replied, looking askance. 'Someone had to do the chores.' She put her head on one side, as if she was wondering whether to tell him something. 'Anyway,' she dismissed, 'I didn't meet many young men, not in my line of work. Only tired social workers and stressed-out doctors.'

She must be lying. You didn't learn the arts of seduction by staying at home scrubbing floors. She could flirt for England—and probably would, given the chance, he thought cynically.

'I can't believe that men weren't attracted to you,' he said, unsettled by the thought of Maddy practising her female arts indiscriminately. To his surprise, she flinched.

'I went out occasionally,' she mumbled. 'Looking after Grandpa had first claim on my time.'

'Do you still look after him?' he shot. 'Wash and clean and shop for him?'

'Of course. He's too old to change and anyway, he's ill now,' she said practically. 'I don't have a job any more so I have to pull my weight. You don't know what it's like to be poor,' she said in a sudden burst of vehemence. 'You've never felt sick at the emptiness of your wallet, or searched around frantically in pockets and down the side of sofas for any spare coins that might buy a few potatoes and some cheese to make a nourishing meal!' Her eyes flashed. 'You've never had to plead with your landlord to let you off this week's rent or had to replace goods at the supermarket checkout because you simply don't have enough to pay the meagre, miserable bill!'

There was a silence while he stared at her, coming to the conclusion that this, at least, must be true.

Clearly angry, she jumped to her feet, took a pan of boiling water from the stove and crashed around with the pans in the sink.

A good deal had become clear in the last few minutes. She was tired of poverty and had seized this chance to leap into the lap of luxury.

Mixed feelings churned around in his brain. Sympathy. Sorrow for the kiddie who'd never known the freedom of childhood—or even those rebellious teenage years. And rage. Hot, seething fury that Cook had used his malleable granddaughter selfishly to make his own life easy—and now to obtain a comfortable old age for himself.

But that didn't change the situation. Marriage was out of the question. No one could ever replace Luisa. He'd never love like that again.

And although Dexter understood Maddy's desperation to marry into a fortune, he felt nothing but contempt for anyone who would put material needs above love and personal integrity.

Nevertheless, he felt a qualm of conscience. When he

told her there was no chance of getting married she would be bitterly disappointed. This was her ticket to paradise and she'd banked everything on it.

Maddy would return as penniless as before. He felt his stomach knot when he thought of the life ahead of her and tried to tell himself that she was just as selfish as old man Cook, that she had no morals and meant to use him as a means to an end.

Yet something drove him to her. Recklessly he strode over to Maddy, putting his arms around her tense, angry body and holding her tight. One of the lamps chose that moment to gutter and die, leaving them in semi-darkness.

'I'm sorry,' he growled. 'Sorry you've had such a hellish life.'

Against his chest, her spine had gone as rigid as a board, her hands motionless in the suds. No. They were shaking. Without thinking, with nothing in his brain but mush, he held her even tighter, his cheek against hers.

'It's been OK. Could have been worse. I wasn't complaining!' she declared, setting to with the pan scourer so fiercely that the pan lurched about in the soapy water, splashing them both with suds.

'Leave that,' he rasped, overwhelmed by a hopeless urge to care for her.

'No!' she yelled, elbowing him away. 'I don't know what came over me. Grandpa and I have had to manage as best we can. We both have our strengths and weaknesses,' she said loyally. 'I'm young and energetic and he's old and sick. That's how it is. I wouldn't dream of moaning about the hand I've been dealt.'

He raised his hands in surrender, the moment of impulse gone. 'OK, OK! But you still want to change your life dramatically, nevertheless.'

'Yes. I do,' she avowed. 'And I will.'

His mouth thinned. Mentally, emotionally, he withdrew his sympathy. She'd do anything for money.

'Really?'

Her solemn gaze met his. She would be different. Oh, she'd still do the chores, but she would get a life, too. And now she'd blown her cover and revealed herself for what she really was—a small-town Cinderella with a washer-woman's hands—she might as well cut her losses, find out what she needed to know and high-tail it out.

'You…haven't had your peaches,' she said jerkily, thinking with stomach-churning dismay that soon they would part and she'd never see him again.

But she wanted to stay. Longed to feel his arms around her again, his mouth on her lips…

Her hungry gaze met his and it was as if a flash sparked between them. His eyes seemed dark and glowing like molten tar and their unexpected expression of longing was making her heart leap about erratically. She'd expected lust. This was more of a…a gentle, hopeless yearning.

Somehow she got up. Stumbled to the bowl on the small dresser. Picked up a plate and a knife and deposited everything safely on the table in front of him.

She hadn't peeled her peach when she'd eaten one earlier. Nor did he. Why should he, when it had grown without sprays and the skin was thin and sensual and deliciously aromatic?

He held it up and she watched him inhaling the scent of sweet, warm sunshine that had been stored in the skin. His eyes closed when his even white teeth sank slowly into the ripe flesh.

Slowly he opened his eyes again and looked at her drowsily from under his lashes while still methodically consuming the peach. It was the most erotic thing she'd ever seen.

She trembled. If she didn't get away from here in a day or so she'd fall under his spell. She *had* to move things on. To ask about the accident.

'Dexter,' she said shakily, 'I want to ask you something important. I must have an answer.'

He stiffened. The desire in his eyes turned to a glittering wariness.

'Ask. You might not like what you hear,' he growled.

'I realise that. But I need to know.' She licked her lips. 'It's about the past—what really happened between our parents.' At his intake of breath, her pleading face lifted to his. 'Grandpa wouldn't tell me anything. He just—'

'Not tonight,' Dexter interrupted tightly, his harrowed face as dark as thunder. He seemed to slump with exhaustion. 'I'm going to bed.'

She stared in dismay as he pushed back his chair. But she could see how weary he was by the angle of his broad shoulders. So she bit back her disappointment. Perhaps they'd talk tomorrow.

'You're tired. I'm sorry,' she said contritely. Leaping to her feet, she added, 'Can I get you anything? A brandy? Some hot chocolate?'

His slow gaze examined her eager-to-help face for a second or two. His mouth took on a sadness that shook her to the core. Then he nodded, his head heavy with fatigue.

'Hot chocolate. Thanks,' he muttered.

Glad to be of use, she hurried to fetch the milk. Out of the corner of her eye she saw Dexter pull some filthy clothes from the bag he'd brought and mechanically stuff them into a laundry basket by the front door.

She frowned. 'You get very dirty in your job.'

'Yes.' Pushing a hand wearily through his hair, he was already heading for the door at the far end of the room.

'But surely you're an executive at least—!'

'Uh.' He turned the handle as though it was an effort. 'Then why—?'

The door banged. She turned to see that he'd closed it behind him. Her heart was bumping. There was something going on that the Fitzgeralds weren't telling her.

Hastily she poured the hot milk over the chocolate powder and followed, intent on solving the mystery. Maybe they'd lost all their money. Maybe all that business with the hotel and smart suits had been a cover-up to hide from their friends the fact that the Quinta was failing and Dex was having to do the manual work himself.

She needed to know. If it was so, then her grandfather would be relieved that she wasn't marrying Dex.

Two doors opened off the narrow corridor. The first was closed, the second was open, the neatly made bed far too feminine for it to be Dexter's. So she knocked on the first.

'Dex?' she called when there was no answer.

Perhaps he was in a bathroom beyond. Cautiously she opened the door a fraction. And saw that he'd fallen, fully clothed, onto the huge double bed. His entire body lay spread-eagled in the relaxed manner of someone deeply, irrevocably, asleep.

She smiled in gentle sympathy and went in, placing the mug of chocolate on a side-table in the sparsely furnished room, and bent to remove his work boots.

He was beautiful. His dark, tousled hair looked rich and glossy against the white of the pillow and a hank of it tumbled on his forehead in such a way that it made her heart turn over.

The black arcs of his thick lashes rested peacefully on the perfectly carved cheekbones and sleep had softened his masculine mouth into a dreamy smile.

Unable to help herself, she reached out and caressed his face with a feather-light touch.

Any other time, any other place, any other situation, she thought wistfully, and she might have fallen for Dexter. Big time.

Confused and agitated by the depth of her attraction, she picked up the mug with shaking fingers and walked out.

Mechanically she poured the chocolate drink down the sink and damped down the fire. Her throat was choked with a huge lump. Because she didn't want to return to her grandfather. Didn't want to remain a spinster.

'You fool!' she muttered wryly. 'You actually *like* the idea of marrying the darn man now!'

How ironic. When she'd fought tooth and nail and had concocted an elaborate pretence to avoid being Mrs Fitzgerald!

It was the biological clock ticking more loudly than ever, she supposed. Though what use was a wife who couldn't have babies? Maybe lots of gorgeous men didn't like the nitty-gritty problems of having children, but not many would positively *hate* their genes to be reproduced. It was a basic urge to have children, wasn't it? Dex would want an heir. Only natural.

Blocking out her feelings, she turned down the wicks of the lamps, picked up her case and hauled it along the corridor to the empty bedroom. She glared at its single bed and stupidly wished she was cuddling up to Dex in the big double, curled like a spoon into his broad back.

Annoyed with herself, she prepared for the coldly virginal bed. Although she kept telling herself that he only saw her as a sex object and that he desired her because she'd played the vamp, her emotions wouldn't listen.

Idiot! He wouldn't be interested in the real Maddy Cook. He wanted boob tubes and snake tattoos, hip swivels and adoring looks from under flapping eyelashes. Shallow. That was what he was.

And if she wanted to keep her emotions from being wrecked, she had to hold him at bay.

CHAPTER EIGHT

THE next morning when she picked up a harloty blouse, she dropped it again mutinously. She'd enjoyed being herself again. And wasn't doing herself up like a dog's dinner again.

In plain shorts and a T-shirt, then, she strode down the corridor, unable to resist a peep as she passed the open door of Dexter's room. It was empty, the bed as pristine as if he'd never slept in it.

She took a deep breath and walked into the living room. Her disappointment on finding it empty too was a revelation.

'You've got it bad, you stupid woman,' she muttered resentfully, and set about making herself some black coffee to jerk her mind into gear.

Nursing the mug, she came to a decision. She'd come clean. Confess to Dex what she'd been up to, pump him for information about their parents, and get herself home before she got hurt.

It was time to stand up to her grandfather; gently but firmly. She had a future to plan. And she intended to show her grandpa that she might be kind and caring but she was strong as well, and quite capable of thinking for herself.

Packing her shoulder bag with goodies, as she had the day before, she set out for the Quinta. It would be a long walk in the merciless sun, but she could do it. And her heart grew light to know that the burden of pretending was about to be removed.

It would be lovely to see the farm again. As she headed

for the hill which hid the main part of the estate from view, she pictured in her mind's eye what she would see. There would be the historic Quinta, of course, sprawling grandly in the centre of the valley, its walls a dazzling white, its gardens a riot of colour. On the terraces maybe a sun umbrella or two, though in the past the back courtyards had been used to dry maize and carob beans and onions.

Her feet hastened up the steep hill as her eagerness increased. There would be flowery meadows full of dragonflies and butterflies. In the nursery there would be rows of gigantic pots brimming with huge stands of palms, bananas, heliconium and all the exotic plants which the residents of the Algarve adored.

The hills would be thick with stone pines, eucalyptus and cork oak. And there would be the orchard, with its luscious oranges and sweet lemons, peaches, apricots...

Her eyes sparkled with anticipation as she paused to take a much-needed breath. Yes. She had adored it here and she had forgotten, the joys of the Quinta being slowly wiped from her mind by the desperation of day-to-day survival in England.

A warm glow curled through her body, followed by a sudden sinking sensation as she realised this could really be the last time she saw Dexter. Ever.

He found it hard to concentrate at work that morning. The pictures in his mind wouldn't stop. The most compelling one was of Maddy's soft concern towards the end of the evening when he'd been unable to hide his exhaustion any longer.

But she'd only been continuing her little angel act, he thought, irritably signing for a delivery of paving slabs. And his enjoyment of her tenderness had been nothing more than his fleeting need to be fussed over. For someone to care.

Fool that he was. His pen dug deep into the paper, making black lines of anger.

By design or accident, she'd pulled all the right strings, wriggling her way into his sympathies with her talk of her lost childhood. But how the hell did he know if she'd been sincere or not? Knowing her agenda, probably not.

Waving away help, he hefted the slabs off the lorry as if to prove to himself that he hadn't gone soft. Yet the pictures persisted, tormenting him.

He kept replaying the events of the evening, seeing over and over again the far-away look in Maddy's eyes and the entrancing sweetness of her face when she'd described what she'd done with her day. Surely a highly coloured version, calculated to hook him.

If so, she'd been successful. Long-dead memories had been brought vividly to life for him. He had gone beyond the pain and his loveless heart had been touched by the images she'd conjured up. OK. Maybe she remembered the Quinta with affection. Much to his surprise, he did too. So what?

Pausing to wipe the sweat from his forehead, he looked around at the barren, blackened land and winced at what he saw. For the first time he acknowledged the distress that the destruction of the farmhouse had caused him.

He'd intended to stay detached. To do the job requested and take off again, his heart untouched. It was easier that way. No feelings equalled no pain.

But Maddy had forced him to listen to her rapturous descriptions and now he could feel the hurt as surely if his own body had been torn in half.

For years he had pretended that this land meant nothing to him—and he'd virtually been convinced. But in reality he'd been protecting himself, ever since he'd fled from his grandmother's vicious tongue. And from the guilt he carried with him to this day of his part in the death of Maddy's parents and his.

Grimly he had made a life for himself that had excluded the place he loved secretly in his heart. He'd kept busy—rather like Maddy—but in his case it hadn't been necessity that had made him work long hours, but the knowledge that if he stopped to think he'd want to return.

And if he did so he would have to relive the accident which had brutally changed his life.

He battled to stall that moment. For now, he had enough on his plate.

And yet he felt compelled to gaze at the ravaged land, unable to stop himself from thinking that Maddy's father and his mother—who'd loved the Quinta more than anyone—would have been in despair over its destruction.

The two families had laboured to turn the old manor house from a ramshackle ruin into a magnificent home. But it had been his mother and Jim Cook who had known every stone and beam, who had harboured a deep and all-consuming love of the farm.

Through them, he and Maddy had learnt to know its moods and to identify the insects, the birds and the plants that colonised the fertile Quinta soil.

The delights of the mellow old Quinta had offered him solace. And a kind of emotional fulfilment. Plus the love of his mother, of course—and that of his grandfather and Jim Cook, all of whom had loved horticulture as he did. The nurturing of plants had been an escape, a balm to the soul, for each one of them.

Perhaps it was the memories of those happy times that had softened his heart and made him susceptible to Maddy's feminine wiles.

He groaned. How he loathed and despised himself for being in an almost permanent state of arousal when she was near!

He'd kept away from women since Luisa had died, three years ago. So much had died inside him, too. He knew he'd become cold and unemotional to protect himself—just as he had as a child.

Yet something about the wholesale ruination of the Quinta had left him a sucker, open to softness and sympathy. He frowned. And something about Maddy had cracked his protective shell even more.

His hand shook. Last night, whilst eating that peach, he'd felt an overpowering desire to take Maddy in his arms and gently kiss her soft lips into submission, to feel the plushness of a woman's body beneath his. To taste ecstasy again.

He had to stop working for a moment because his breathing was so laboured. But he shouldn't feel like this about someone so superficial and materialistic. That domestic angel he'd seen last night was a mirage. She wasn't like that at all—no matter how badly he wanted her to be that mirage, that angel.

With dismay, he realised that he missed Luisa more than he'd thought. For some reason he'd been unconsciously searching for someone to replace her. As if anyone ever could.

For she had been sweet and gentle and as honest as the day was long. Even to look at her had given him a warm feeling inside. Her face...

He felt himself tense up. In vain he tried to recall her appearance. Another image kept getting in the way. A woman with bright, silvered eyes that could change to darkest charcoal and completely drown him. Whose smile beckoned and lured like that of a siren. Who made him laugh and rage and wonder in the space of a few minutes. *Maddy*.

And yet she wasn't worth one hair of Luisa's head. His eyes watered and a lump came to his throat. His Luisa had been ripped from his mind and replaced by a harlot. He shouldn't even sully his late wife's memory by even thinking of her in the same breath!

'She's a money-grabbing hooker! Remember that, you idiot!' he muttered angrily under his breath.

Riven with anger and self-loathing, he dropped a paving stone and cracked it. His booted foot kicked it viciously aside and he wondered what would have happened if she hadn't mentioned their parents' accident. His moment of mad longing for her had been brought to a shuddering halt and his rampant hormones had gone into free fall.

'Boss? You all right?'

He glared at Manuel, his manager. 'What the hell do you think?' he flared. And then groaned, waving a hand in apology. 'I'm sorry, Manuel. Forgive me. Inexcusable.'

His manager's face was gentle and understanding. 'Bad time, boss. We feel it hard. You...' He shrugged as if to express his sympathy, then put his hand on Dex's arm. 'Sorry to tell you this. Last chance to search the house. Four hours till the bulldozers move in.'

Dexter felt his chest tighten. 'Right. Don't pull any men off,' he muttered. 'I want to be on my own.'

He strode purposefully to the ruins of the house. This was it. A final goodbye. Soon there would be nothing left of the memories that crowded into his mind.

The good and the bad. The two grandfathers, increasingly pulling in opposite directions because of their vastly different characters and strutting about like stallions, shouting at one another whilst he and Maddy leapt out of their way.

The happiness he'd felt when he'd worked in the nursery, helping Jim Cook—and how ironically he'd often wished at that time that Jim had been his father.

His mother, white-faced and haunted as she'd kissed him that dark day when he was fifteen, her hair soft and fragrant on his face when she'd enveloped him in her arms and husked an emotional goodbye.

He hadn't known then that it had been a final farewell, that she'd intended to escape his father's bullying and run off with Jim Cook. He hadn't known that it would be the last time he saw her alive.

It hurt. Dear heaven, how it hurt. Suppressing a sharp spasm of pain, he put on his tough working gloves and bent to rummage in the chaos that had once been his home.

Full of anticipation, Maddy crested the hill. And immediately she froze as if turned to stone.

Her legs suddenly gave way beneath her and she crumpled to the soft green turf, staring in horror and clutching at her chest as the breath jerked in harsh and laboured gasps.

'No!' she croaked, trying to deny the undeniable. *'No!'*

Her mind whirled as she struggled to make sense of the terrible scene. A devastating forest fire had clearly roared over the estate, stopping only at the foot of the hill where she sat. Below her she could see a wide trench that must have been a hastily constructed fire break. It had saved the western part of the Quinta land from fire damage, but not the major part of the estate.

Reaching out shakily, she grasped at the emerald turf for some kind of solid reassurance. Beside her, behind her, the sweet and verdant land offered untold delights to the eyes. Ahead there was nothing but desolation.

At first sight it seemed that everything was black, but

then she began to make out the heaps of grey ash that once must have been living plants. And there were incongruously gaudy orange diggers working in the centre of the plain where the Quinta had once stood.

Her hand flew to her mouth in horror. The beautiful farmhouse had been utterly ruined.

Everything she'd remembered so vividly and so lovingly had been destroyed. All her happy memories had been wiped away and, with them, a part of herself had gone too. Everything the Quinta had represented—those tender moments with her father and her deep love of the land—had been cruelly obliterated.

She gave a plaintive cry that came right from the depths of her being.

'Oh, *Dex!*'

No wonder he'd been preoccupied. Curt. Unwilling to bend his mind to being sociable towards his proposed bride. Awash with misery, she shaded her eyes, realising he would be out there now, working to clear the land. And her heart went out to him. She understood his pain. However emotional she was feeling about the terrible scene, it must be ten times worse for him.

She'd loved the Quinta. But it had been Dex's entire life.

Long-suppressed tears began to roll down her face. She had to go to him. To say how she felt, that she understood.

Sobbing, driven on by her desire to comfort him somehow, she stumbled down the hill, towards the ugly blackness.

The sun burned down remorselessly. His chest felt hollow, as if an emptiness had begun to spread through his body.

He'd been working for perhaps an hour. His eyes prickled and he scowled ferociously at the blackened mess. This was hopeless. There was nothing worth saving. What was the point? He was looking for something he'd never find.

Love. Peace of mind. Tenderness.

Damn Maddy Cook for stirring up his emotions! Curse her wine-dyed hair for making him want what he could never have!

'Dex!'

His whole body jerked at the sound of her shocked gasp and then he sprang up from his crouching position to face her, white-hot with fury that she should invade his space at this deeply personal moment.

'What the hell are you doing here?' he roared in hoarse fury.

For a split-second she thought that he meant to hit her. His fists were clenched and his body hunched menacingly in a physical threat.

Shaky from the long trek and the shock of what she'd seen, she lost her footing. Fell onto the tarry ground and winced at the horrible crunch of charcoaled wood and plant matter as it crumbled beneath her.

Brushing herself down, her face now smudged like a chimney sweep's, she slowly rose to her feet.

And then she saw him clearly. He was grey with despair. His black eyes blazing in a bitter fury at what had happened to the Quinta.

'Oh, Dex!' she whispered hopelessly.

Misery twisted his mouth. A look of utter bleakness collapsed all the muscles of his face before he hastily turned away and ripped savagely at a carbonised beam which was sitting drunkenly on what remained of a stone wall.

For a moment she closed her eyes, because she couldn't bear to see him so desperately unhappy. She wanted to help him. To make everything all right again. But knew she couldn't.

And, because of her helplessness, the tears began to fall down her cheeks again.

'Dex!' she mumbled brokenly, watching in despair as his rage unleashed itself on the charred timbers of his home. 'I'm so sorry. It's awful. Nothing in my wildest dreams prepared me for this. I—I can't believe what's happened. Was…was anyone hurt?'

'No!'

She flinched at his abruptness. The old Maddy would have muttered something and hurried away with her tail between her legs. But she couldn't leave without knowing what had happened. Too often she'd remained unquestioning over important matters. She knew that only led to a torment of uncertainty that scoured away at her, keeping her awake at night.

So she braved his angry and uncompromising figure and trampled grimly over piles of debris till she'd come close enough to speak without shouting.

'I don't understand,' she said chokily. 'The house was built of stone but there's little of it left—'

'That's because of the wood in its construction,' he growled curtly, pushing away a heap of rubble in exasperation. 'The roof. The floors. Lintels and doors. They burned and weakened the stone. In any case, the heat was intense. The gas cylinders at the back of the kitchen exploded.'

She shivered in horror, cringing at the thought of an entire house being burnt to the ground. Her home. His. All she could see were a few remnants of the outer wall and the huge, solid chimney, some large timbers and heaps of tangled, blackened stuff that must be all that was left of the family furniture and possessions.

Incongruously, in the far corner where the kitchen had been, a buckled steel fridge reared out of the piles of soot and charred wood. Her eyes darted about. There were partly

melted saucepans. An iron bath that had fallen to the
ground floor and now lurched precariously against the man-
gled remains of the wrought-iron balcony. Over it all rose
a stench of soot and smoke. Already her throat felt sore
from it.

She mopped her face, hot and sweaty from the long walk
and the heat of the scorched earth.

'It's appalling,' she whispered. 'How can you bear it?'

The broad back expanded with a huge intake of breath.
'You think I have any choice?' he bit.

He shot a cold, malevolent look over his shoulder.

'I'm sorry. I'm sorry, that was stupid,' she mumbled, her
hands twisting helplessly together. 'I don't know what to
say—'

'Then don't.' He took a longer look at her and she was
very conscious of her dishevelled appearance. Her face
must be scarlet from the heat and sweat was making her
clothes cling to her in a totally unbecoming way. To say
nothing of the streaks of soot everywhere. He frowned.
'Did you walk here?'

When she'd first climbed into his truck on the day she'd
arrived he'd talked of a fire, she recalled with a jerk. It
must have happened some days ago...

She cringed. And all the while she'd been batting her
eyelashes at him and cavorting around at the hotel... It was
too awful. What must he have thought of her?

'Yes,' she choked, not knowing where to start with her
apologies. 'I—I came to see you—'

'Is that a fact?' he sneered. 'I think you wanted to see
the Quinta,' he grated. His eyes seared hers, glittering with
a terrible anger. 'Your *dowry*.'

She went white. 'No! That is, I wanted to see it, of
course—'

'Yeah. Of *course*,' he growled, extending his arm mockingly as if introducing the wreckage to her. 'Well, here it is.'

She trembled, bewildered and frightened by the darkness of his fury. And ached to console him. But the gap between them was more than the foot or so that separated their two bodies. He had wrapped himself in a murderous hatred of the fire that only his frantic physical assault on the ruins of the farmhouse could possibly appease.

Maddy was more deeply upset than she could ever have imagined. The gardens which had graced the long drive up to the Quinta had been obliterated by the fire. The two grandfathers had planted oleander and bougainvillaea, hibiscus and datura, exotic palms and bananas. Specimen shrubs from all over the world had been incorporated into the design. It had been the talk of the Algarve and the imaginative planting had brought garden lovers to the garden centre from far afield. Now just a few miserable trunks of blackened palms bore witness to its former glory.

'There must have been thousands of plants here,' she choked.

'My life's work!' he rasped.

'Dexter!' she gasped.

She wanted to touch him. To console him. And he was blocking her out. That hurt so much.

It was terrible to see the virulence of his rage. He lifted the blackened oak beams as if they weighed nothing, his muscles bulging with effort, the veins in his neck standing out.

Sweat had formed a dark, sticky V on his back and begrimed his face, and he only paused to flick an impatient gloved hand at it when it began to trickle into his eyes.

And those eyes! She cringed at their expression. It was as though he was in a deep hole of hell. Her tender heart

ached for him. He'd lost everything, she thought in horror.
No wonder Sofia had been grimmer than usual.

'Are you…ruined, Dex?' she breathed timidly.

He whirled around, his mouth grim, a fearsome glitter in
his eyes.

'What if I am?' he snapped.

Her face crumpled at her inability to find words of
comfort.

'It…it would be dreadful!' she stammered.

'Wouldn't it just?' he snarled.

Although she flinched, she could understand his bitterness. It must have been the most terrible shock. Distressed
for him, she tried to collect her thoughts together.

He turned his back on her again, but she felt that she
had to tell him how she felt. He needed to know that she
cared and if he needed her…

Wanting to be needed more than anything, she gulped,
fiercely suppressing the tears which threatened to render her
incoherent again. She had to tell him how she felt, that she
shared some of his pain.

'I couldn't believe my eyes,' she said shakily. 'I was
expecting to see trees and meadows and rows of plants in
the nursery. Instead, I saw…I saw that everything was
burnt and charred.' Her voice wobbled as she relived the
horror, and then her frantic desperation to find Dex and to
express her compassion. 'It was horrible to walk across
what had once been fields,' she jerked. 'The grass crackled
beneath my feet and broke. Every step I took sent up clouds
of soot.' She gave a shudder. 'I think the acrid smell will
stay with me for ever. So much, reduced to ashes,' she
whispered, reliving that nightmare journey in the merciless
sun, every painful, miserable step. 'And—and this…the
Quinta…'

She couldn't voice her feelings properly. A huge lump

of emotion had risen to block her throat and tears were hot
and prickling at the backs of her eyelids once more.

Dexter stopped viciously hurling timber out of his way
and stood there glaring at her, cold and tight-jawed, sooty
smears on his forehead and cheeks.

'Yes. All gone,' he said curtly. 'Not a stick of antique
furniture left. Not one valuable oil painting…'

Aghast, she clutched at her chest to hold in her frantically
pulsing heart.

'Couldn't you save anything?'

That earned her a scathing look so vitriolic that she felt
as if he'd stabbed her. Why? she wondered in bewilderment. Why so angry with her?

'I wasn't here,' he said tightly. 'They got my grandmother out and then all the staff concentrated on saving the
horses and the other animals. The more important things,'
he said scathingly. 'By the time they got back to the house
it was too dangerous to enter.' His mouth became cruel and
thin. 'So there are no treasures saved for you, Maddy.'

She bit her lip, uncomprehending as she met his cold
eyes. Feeling sick, she realised that there was nothing between them. Never had been, never would be. His kiss had
been driven by lust. She was there, apparently available,
and he'd taken what he thought was on offer.

Misery and fatigue pervaded her entire body and she
sank to the ground on her knees, unable to stand. Debris
dug into her legs but she didn't care.

'If you weren't here, where were you? When did you get
here?' she jerked.

'I flew from Brazil immediately when I heard,' he said
shortly. 'About a week ago.'

'Brazil?' she repeated stupidly.

He rasped in a harsh breath. 'I'm a plant hunter. I roam
the world searching for new varieties, new producers.'

She tried to understand but her mind seemed stuck.

'You don't—didn't—live here with your grandmother?'

'I— What the hell does it matter?' he snarled. 'Apart from a few short years, I haven't lived here since my parents' funeral, if you want to know.'

Her eyes widened. 'You were fifteen, for goodness' sake! Where did you go?'

He gave an exasperated growl but he answered, much to her surprise. 'I ran away to Lisbon and got a job on a ship washing decks. I didn't come back until five years later, when I discovered that my grandfather had died and there was talk that the farm was to be put up for sale. I pulled it back to life again as fast as I could,' he said grimly. 'And then I put in a good manager and went back to my travels. Grandmama and I don't see eye to eye. Is that enough for you?' he snapped brutally. 'Now, let me get on. I can't waste time. Go away. You're filthy already. See one of the men. They'll give you a lift back.'

Maddy looked at herself. Her trainers were black from walking across the scorched and forsaken fields. Her legs were grimy, her shorts smeared with soot.

'This is why you were dirty when we first met,' she said in a low tone. 'Why you've been working so many hours a day—and why you were so foul-tempered when you picked me up at the airport! Why didn't you tell me?' she cried in sudden irritation. 'Why?'

'Why the hell should I?' he rasped, on his knees and reaching beneath a tangle of twisted metal. 'We told your grandfather,' came his muffled voice. 'He chose not to tell you. Why should we question his decision?' he added savagely.

Her eyes widened. 'But…why didn't *he* tell me?' she asked shakily, remembering how Dex had laughed and remarked that her grandfather had made a fool of her.

'Would you have come?' Dexter asked coldly.

'No. Of course not,' she whispered, her throat dry and scratchy.

'That's what *he* thought,' Dexter scathed.

'But how *could* you all have kept this from me?' she protested in distress.

He straightened up and walked over to where he'd placed a water bottle and took a long drink from it before answering.

'If you'd known that the Quinta and the entire business had gone up in flames you would have stayed at home. And he couldn't let you do that. Not with a wealthy husband in the offing. Admit it, Maddy. You don't care about the farm at all. Only its value in monetary terms.'

She drew in a huge, shuddering gasp of outrage, her eyes blazing with icy silver lights. And she leapt up and launched herself at him, pummelling his chest in frustrated fury.

'Listen to me! Listen! I do care! I'm upset—!'

He wrenched himself away and exploded. In a furious action he grabbed her arm then bent down and grabbed a handful of charred material, thrusting it in front of her nose.

'Look at it!' he roared. 'To you, this represents a luxury you have lost. Rich furnishings. The trappings of wealth. But to me, it's my heart and soul and guts! I made the Quinta a household name in Portugal. My blood and sweat and tears have gone into this! I know where every plant came from. Every seed, every cutting, every lovingly nurtured graft. Years of work and dedication have gone into the success of this nursery. That's what I've lost! That and...' He stopped, his voice too hoarse to continue for a moment. And then he blazed, 'You say you *care*? What do *you* know about feelings?'

'Everything!' she sobbed. 'Don't shut me out, Dex, I can't bear it—'

'Get away from here!' he snarled. 'I've got three hours to find something, anything that once belonged to my mother, and I don't want you around.'

'But I can help! Let me help you!' she begged croakily. *'No!'*

Seething with anger, he foraged grimly in the tangled remains of what must have been the main living room, where the huge chimney still remained.

Stubbornly she ignored him. Found a spot out of his way. Got on her knees and began a fingertip search, hoping and praying that she would find something for him and earn his praise. She wanted that so very much. Was desperate to ease his bitter anger.

It was a long while, perhaps more than two hours, before he noticed her. Faint and dizzy from the heat, she heard him scramble to his feet, muttering. There was the now familiar ghastly crunch of his feet as he walked stiffly to the water bottle. And then she heard him approaching her.

Cringing, she waited for his tirade of abuse, determined to let it wash over her. Yet already she'd begun to weep, her aching and exhausted body shaking with her choking sobs.

Something nudged her shoulder. She dashed the filthy back of her hand across her eyes and saw it was the water bottle. Meekly she took it and sat back on her haunches, sipping the cool spring water with gratitude.

'Look at you!' growled Dexter roughly. 'Why are you so bull-headed? You do what you want and to hell with everyone else.' He pulled at her arm. 'Call it a day,' he ordered curtly.

'No! I haven't found anything!' she yelled hoarsely, resisting with all her might.

'Neither have I,' he snapped. 'But I can't hold back the bulldozers any longer.'

Her eyes rounded in horror. 'Oh, no, Dex!' she croaked.

'Get up!' he snarled.

He was too strong for her. She found herself being hauled to her feet and pulled away from the remains of the Quinta. He waved his arm and there was the sound of a mighty roar as the digger and bulldozer were started up simultaneously.

Half stumbling over the uneven ground in Dexter's ruthless grip, half in mid-air when he grew impatient with her faltering progress and hurried her along with his hands beneath her armpits, she felt waves of dizziness spiralling inexorably through her body.

'*Please!* I can't go on!' she gasped, and was suddenly released, to crumple in a boneless heap on the ground.

Water was being poured over her head. She lifted her face to the silver stream, glad of its coolness. As rigid as an iron bar, Dexter came to sit a few feet away. Instantly she forgot her own misery and tuned in to his.

The tightness of his jaw was so extreme that she thought his muscles would go into spasm. He stared hollow-eyed at the bulldozer as it trundled closer and closer to the ruined Quinta.

He was barely breathing at all, his eyes stabbed with pain. Tentatively she put a trembling hand on his arm and was glad when he didn't shake it off. Her eyes never left his. She heard the chimney collapse and her grip tightened when he flinched as if it had been a physical blow to his stomach. But she had to give him hope, however tenuous.

'It's not the end. You can do it again. Build up the business,' she said, over the noise of the digger scooping up stone and debris.

There was a huge expansion of his chest with his ragged

intake of breath. Still he didn't speak. Maddy swallowed. What could she do or say? Dexter didn't want her around at all—and no wonder.

He had more than enough to deal with and it must have infuriated him that he'd had to dance attendance on her at such a difficult time.

'I'm sorry,' she muttered hopelessly. 'I'm so sorry.'

Drowning her words, trucks thundered past, carrying the spoil. They watched in numbed silence as the battered, twisted and burned remains of Dexter's family home were scooped up and transported to the huge skips.

And suddenly everything went quiet again. With her eyes blurred by tears, she looked around and saw that there was nothing left of the historic farmhouse. Slowly she and Dexter got to their feet.

'Manuel!' he called huskily and a man hurried over.

'Boss?'

'I'm taking her away. You know what to do.'

'Sure,' came the soft reply. 'See you tomorrow.'

Dexter nodded dumbly.

'She using the showers?' Manuel asked.

A brief snort. 'A little public, even for her,' he said wearily.

'You don't have to take me back,' she mumbled, as his hand curled around her elbow. 'I can walk back. Save you the bother—'

'You'll do as you're told!' he spat.

She bit her lip. His emotions were so highly charged that she dared not contradict him. And she had to admit that she wanted to get far away from this dark and evil place and see the soft green countryside again.

Now the machines were silenced, and the men were taking a break, she realised that an unnatural quiet had fallen.

There was no birdsong in this bleak and terrible land. Just desolation.

She couldn't contain her sobs. They racked her body so violently that she couldn't move. Dexter suddenly muttered a low curse and swept her up in his arms. But there was nothing romantic or caring about the action.

Irritation and hatred were driving him to get rid of her as fast as he could, because she was only someone who'd warm his bed and give him children. Nothing more. Every hard, unforgiving bone and muscle in his body told her that.

Inconsolable with grief, she curled into a ball against his chest, her fists clenched tightly. And she knew then that she wanted his respect and friendship more than anything in the world. But would never have it.

CHAPTER NINE

IT CAME close to being the worst day of his life. Clenching his jaw, he stifled the emotion which was trying to burst out of him and carried her to where the cars and trucks were parked.

In his arms she seemed frail and vulnerable, a desperately pathetic figure. Sure she was distraught, he thought, dragging out his keys from his pocket. She'd lost the chance of untold wealth, hadn't she?

His muscles tensed as the crackling fury surged through his body. What was her self-centred misery compared to his? How could she ever know what it did to him, seeing this ravaged land that had once been a paradise on earth?

He remembered his mother's delight when the business had made enough money to enable them to buy antique furniture. How she'd danced around the terrace with him after it had been delivered. The scent of her. His happiness.

Without speaking, he wrenched open the door of his car and pushed her in, slamming the door viciously. When he flung himself in beside her, his malevolent glance in her direction told him that she was still weeping quietly to herself, her face white beneath the streaks of soot.

Impatiently he snapped her into the seat belt, jammed his own into its slot, and gunned the engine.

Usually careful of his sleek drop-head, he accelerated so fast in his anger that he had to fight the wheel as the car skidded on the loose soil.

He had to get away. To see something green and soothing to the eyes. The bleakness of the landscape around the farm only added to his depression, and whenever he could he avoided even driving along the main road where the fire damage was visible, taking the back roads instead.

This time he was in a hurry. Maddy had to get cleaned up and then he'd take her to the airport, whether she liked it or not.

She gave a particularly heart-rending sob and he shot her a quick glance. He felt a clutch of pain in his chest. It seemed to be some kind of alarm signal, perhaps, warning him that things weren't right with her. She was shivering, her eyes blankly staring ahead, her hands twisting and knotting in her lap.

Shock, he thought in contempt. You see a multimillion fortune a hand's reach away and then it disappears. Enough to send any self-respecting greedy little gold-digger into shock.

But despite his contempt he took the pot-holed road to the cottage more slowly than he'd intended and tried to hold back his temper. Whatever the reason, however shallow it might be, she looked terrible.

When they stopped and he burst from the car, she remained in her seat as if paralysed. Ignoring her miserable, wan expression, he stayed by the door to the cottage. He wouldn't touch her unless absolutely necessary.

'Get out.'

Maddy jerked at his harsh bark, her eyes huge and shining with tears. As if her limbs were stiff and aching, she climbed slowly out. And then, clearly realising how filthy she was for the first time, she gave a little moan and tried to brush the worst of the soot and dust from her clothes.

'I wish this was a five-star hotel,' she muttered miserably.

He couldn't believe what she'd said. He was in the middle of a nightmare and she was moaning about her creature comforts!

'They'd never let you in like that,' he snarled.

She pursed her lips. 'No. They wouldn't,' she agreed faintly. 'But right at this moment I'd give anything just to leap into a bath.'

Impatiently he moved forward and caught her arm, drawing her into the cottage. He left her in the middle of the room.

No longer was she the flirty siren who'd once tried to entice him into a disastrous alliance, but a filthy beggar woman with black streaks down her face, soot and mud ingrained in her hands and nails, and with knees and legs the colour of charcoal.

She caught his look of disgust and contempt and blanched. Cynically he watched her swaying—and then realised she really was physically exhausted.

'Damn you!' he muttered, and grabbed her just as her knees gave way.

'Don't be angry with me, Dex!' she pleaded.

Her helpless, upturned face made his guts churn. Those spaniel eyes with their black, spiky lashes took hold of his innards and twisted them till he felt himself softening.

Until he hardened his heart. Held her at arm's length and pushed her to the sofa.

'Wait there,' he growled, his entire body seething with intense loathing.

Her soulful eyes met his and he flinched. Were his as raw as that? Were they bleak and hurt too?

'Dex,' she whispered, her voice breaking into a sob.

'I'll heat some water,' he rasped, his voice hoarse and cracked.

More tears from her. For a stupid, faltering moment he watched them fill her eyes and overflow. Something drew him to her, something intangible and irrational, and it took all his will-power to resist it.

He was weak. So overwhelmed by emotion that a harlot's tears could evoke pity.

This upsurge of feelings was something he'd always guarded against. He wanted to be detached again. To think of work and nothing else. To enjoy each day and its simple pleasures without his head being tangled with a jumble of thoughts and yearnings.

Stonily he crashed pans about and filled them with water. Stoked up the stove. Boiled the kettle, threw her a blanket and managed to avoid helping her to wrap it around herself, even when she struggled with its folds.

His hands shook when he took the mug of tea to her.

'Here.' He thrust it at her without ceremony.

Up went her beseeching eyes, causing turmoil in his chest.

'Dex,' she breathed shakily, the tea slopping in her trembling hands. 'Take it easy on yourself—'

'Stay out of my life,' he snapped, turning his back on her.

There was the sound of crying again. Unable to stand it, he stormed off to fetch the huge tin bath. After placing it close to the stove, he stripped off his T-shirt and washed his hands and face at the basin, using water from the kettle.

The pans were boiling. Gradually he filled the bath with hot water. Added some cold when it was deep enough. Flicked her a sour glance. Hell. She was trembling like a leaf.

'It's ready,' he said curtly. 'Here's the soap. Get cleaned up.'

Busily refilling the pans for his own bath, he heard the sounds. The whisper of clothes being shrugged off, the soft thump as they dropped to the floor. A foot testing the water.

He felt an odd constriction in his chest. The hairs rose on the back of his neck. There was a silence. Yet he could almost hear her shaking.

'Hurry up,' he ordered, hoping to urge her on, to jolt her out of her state of shock and to send her on her way.

'I am!' she flung unhappily.

He heard the sound of furious lathering. Somehow he finished cleaning the sink, though his ears were attuned all the time to the splashes of water. He dried his hands and flung down the towel, taking a furious step in the direction of his bedroom.

There was a shaky little gasp behind him and somehow his stride turned it into a movement that had him spinning around to stare at Maddy with cold fury because she was breaking his resolve.

He felt his mind lurching uncontrollably between loathing and despising her...and desiring every luscious inch. Those fragile shoulder blades, the achingly small waist. Her dark burgundy hair tousled. Huge, smoky eyes awash with tears, heart-shaped face tragic in its misery. The beautiful mouth... Dexter clenched his teeth together as if that might stop him from wanting to kiss it.

Or to touch those high, rounded breasts and to feel their peaks tighten and swell beneath his fingers...

Her hands had stilled and she was gazing at him with enormous, infuriatingly appealing eyes. He could hardly breathe. Pressure was building in his lungs.

'Get on with it,' he said.

And dragged breath into his aroused body. He knew what she was, how much he hated her. And yet she had invaded every pore, flowed in every vein, her face and wheedling eyes and her sensual curves filling his head with an irresistible lure. Which he must resist—or use her as she meant to use him.

'I am trying to,' she whispered.

Maddy's hands slid soapily over her body. She felt languorous and seductive. Someone groaned—it could have been her. Opening her eyes, she found herself lost in awe of his dark and brooding eyes. Her hands covered her breasts in a belated modesty.

Her eyes asked him to take one stride forward so that her arms could encircle his strong neck and she could kiss away his despair. She found herself struggling for breath. But she needed to speak. He was in such anguish and she wanted to ease it.

'Dex,' she whispered tenderly. 'I know why you're so angry. But give in to your grief, don't bottle it up. There's no shame in what you feel. You have gone out to the Quinta day after day and that nightmare scene of blackened earth has been driven into your brain. That terrible, soulless world must have dominated your mind, waking and sleeping,' she soothed as he stood there without moving a muscle, totally transfixed by her words. 'It would crack even the hardest heart to see the devastation—and you love the farm so much. It's terrible that it's not the same place any more. Even the sounds are different. Not a single bleat from a goat or sheep,' she reflected. 'No bustle and scurry of hens or the whinny of ponies. Just the machinery, droning on and on relentlessly. I *know* how you feel—'

'Yeah? How?' he grated, his agonisingly pained eyes flashing like jet.

'Because I knew how my father felt when one of his plants died after he'd nurtured and tended it,' she answered passionately. 'Because I remember how animated you used to become when Dad talked to you about the nursery and his plans for it. I know that the loss of your stock is more than merely a commercial blow—'

'That's enough!' he rasped. And he turned his back on her, feverishly collecting up her clothes.

Miserable that he was rejecting her attempts to help, she slowly soaped her breasts. Astonished, she found that they were swollen and tender. Her fingers swept across her nipples and starbursts of pleasure rocketed through her body, bringing a hot flush of shame and embarrassment to her skin.

Looking up guiltily, she found that he had turned to watch, sardonic and glowering, his eyes slivered with derision. Excitement flashed through her like lightning, stimulating every susceptible inch.

Again she wrapped her arms around herself in protection, horrified by the wicked longings that urged her to slide herself against him and demand to be kissed.

'I want...' Her throat closed at the blazing light in his eyes, the force of electricity that suddenly charged the air between them. She tried again. 'I want...a...towel, please,' she stumbled incoherently.

Tight-lipped, he strode out and reappeared a moment later with one. She stepped out, frantically trying to cover herself, and he flung the towel at her then dragged the tub out to empty it. The pans on the stove filled the room with steam.

He filled the tub and then his glance met hers again. It seemed they couldn't take their eyes off one another. With slow and heavy movements she sought to fight off the sensual lassitude that had loosened her body and she did her best to rub herself dry. But with Dexter watching her so avidly she found her hands slowing until they were exacerbating her arousal instead of briskly easing it.

Holding her gaze, he undid his belt. Stepped out of his trousers and then his briefs. Maddy didn't turn away. She felt panic and a delicious anticipation coiling in her stomach as he stepped into the tub and sat down.

He wanted her. That was more than obvious. For a moment she'd seen how fiercely aroused he was, and then she had hastily looked away, retaining an image of male beauty that made her body ache.

'Wash my back, would you?' he husked harshly.

As if in a dream, she tucked the towel around her securely and knelt by the side of the tub. Picking up the soap, she kept her eyes fixed on his torso, too nervous to look elsewhere.

His back was beautiful. Quite perfect; a broad triangle of gleaming muscle narrowing to a small waist and hips. Her hands learned him, lovingly lathering his shoulders and marvelling at the powerful bulge of his biceps.

His hand lifted to catch hold of her face, caressing it wonderingly. And then his mouth was crushing hers and everything in her head seemed to break into fragments.

Somehow she was in the water again, naked, her legs wrapped around his back. His kisses rained on her lips, fierce and passionate, his hands gently stroking her quivering breasts.

'Dex!' she whispered, and found her mouth invaded by his tongue, which moved so erotically that she thought she might faint with pleasure.

It seemed that she was on fire, the urges of her body making her slide close to him and gasp at the hardness that reared against her. His head dipped and she moaned as his mouth closed over each nipple in turn, fanning the flames in her hungry body till she was forced to writhe sinuously in her desperate need.

'Harlot,' he growled, his eyes blazing with fires of their own.

She blinked, startled and bewildered, and then sank,

gasping, in his arms. For he had touched her where she most longed to be touched, his slippery fingers moving with wickedly expert delicacy whilst she whimpered with the indescribable pleasure.

She seemed to experience an explosion inside her, her body elongating as it stretched sensuously against his. And she felt an overwhelming surge of power and need, kissing him fiercely, not caring that his hard, demanding mouth might bruise her soft lips or that his teeth seemed clenched in an incomprehensible anger.

With an imprecation muttered hoarsely under his breath, he pulled her upright and carried her wilting, throbbing body to his bedroom, throwing her on the bed as if she were truly the harlot he imagined.

She had to tell him, she thought dazedly. And then his body covered hers and she knew this was all that she wanted, all she'd ever dreamed of. A man as strong and dynamic as Dexter and who loved the land with an overwhelming passion. Who could kiss her stupid and touch...

'Oh, there!' she whispered, bucking beneath him.

'Maddy,' he muttered into her mouth. 'Maddy, Maddy!'

He paused, shaking. Lazily she opened her eyes in an impatient question.

'What is it?' she slurred.

'Are you safe?'

She nodded dumbly. There was no chance that she would get pregnant. For a brief moment his eyes narrowed in scorn and she was scared, thinking he meant to draw away. So she arched her body, wantonly moving her hands over her breasts. And he gave a groan, his mouth sweetly tugging, fingers remorselessly tormenting.

Warmth filled her. A hard, silky, pulsing warmth that made her bite her lip as her loins melted around it and the core of her body tightened greedily in welcome.

'Yes,' she mumbled, her head thrashing on the pillow. *'Yes!'*

He felt his whole body jerk in primitive response, found himself surrendering to the rhythm that united them. He wanted to think. But there was too much emotion ricocheting around his head and body, all of it provoked and aroused by the sweetly scented, sensual woman who was crying out his name and rendering him senseless with hot, carnal desire.

His mind blanked. There was nothing but the sound of their panting and their moans, the never-ending pleasure that filled every corner of his empty body and brought it to shocking, exultant life.

He cried out too. Clasped her hard, kissed her till he felt dizzy, tried—dear heaven, how he tried!—to take her into himself, to join her flesh with his so that every physical barrier had been removed and all that remained was the liquid flow of his heart into hers.

She shuddered throughout her body, gave a gasping cry and became still just as he erupted inside her, the sweetness of it almost unbearable. Muttering her name quietly to himself, he held her in a close embrace.

And he knew with a sinking feeling of dismay that he had given something to her that was not only physical but also an essential part of him.

It had all been a terrible mistake. He should have remained cold and detached. Anything other than a purely physical response was wasted on her.

Gently she stroked his face and, like the fool he was, he wanted it to go on for ever. To pretend that she wasn't a grasping little whore, who'd been prepared to prostitute herself for money, but the tender and loving person he had once known.

His teeth clenched. Who was he kidding? He rolled over

and glared at her, determined to kill his emotions stone-dead.

'Whatever will Grandpa say?' he drawled with deliberate cruelty. It gave him a bitter pleasure that she gasped and flinched in dismay. 'Sex without marriage,' he mocked. 'Tut-tut. I think your plan has backfired, Maddy.'

But he couldn't help kissing her. That mouth pouted so effectively, luring him with its plushness. And he felt himself weakening, the bones in his body liquefying as she moaned and wrapped her body skilfully around his.

'You're wrong. My plan worked,' she whispered sadly.

'Sure,' he croaked, extricating himself and trying to contain the shafts of desire stabbing at his chest. 'Here we are, married.'

'Dex!' she breathed in distress. 'You don't understand...' She choked and didn't finish the sentence.

'We had sex. That's all.'

Cold with anger at himself, he flung himself from the bed and twisted a towel around his waist.

Maddy took a deep breath, her eyes wounded. For a moment she'd thought they'd shared something special. And she'd been terribly, stupidly wrong.

She felt sick that she'd been so easily seduced. He must be thinking that she was a push-over.

Face aflame with humiliation, close to tears of misery, she began unravelling herself from the tangled sheets, intending to make a dignified exit.

'I don't know why you're so angry,' she said jerkily, swinging her legs to the floor. '*You* used *me*—'

His hand arrested her progress. 'Yes, and why not? You were intent on using me!' he snarled. 'You wanted me for my money.'

His words lanced into her like a sword. She'd got herself

into this with her silly plan. And he'd had no qualms about taking what he'd wanted.

'And you wanted sex!'

'Sure I did. It was on offer, wasn't it?' he derided.

Her lip trembled. For the first time in her life she had felt pure, perfect bliss. But for him it had been lust, the corruption of human love. And he thought carnal desire would be sufficient for a marriage.

With a sob of horror, she escaped to her bedroom, hastily washed herself with cold water from the ewer on the wash-stand and pulled on her blue dress. She flung her case onto the bed and began to sort out her things.

In jeans and T-shirt, he stalked in, a glass of wine in his hand. Her heart did a flip and she had to force herself not to fling herself into his arms so that she could feel him, touch him, be close to him again. Her brain was turned, she thought glumly.

'So. You're packing,' he said, his tone as cold as ice.

Her head whirling with hopeless longing, she turned away to conceal her wince of pain.

Tough it out, she told herself. She'd had her adventure and some of it had been fun. Time to set the record straight, ask a few questions and make her way home.

She shuddered. It alarmed her that the thought of the cramped flat and her grandfather's lashing tongue should be even more unappealing than usual. But she had no choice. She'd managed before, she would now. And she was a different person.

'Observant of you,' she scathed uncharacteristically. 'Must be those laser eyes.'

'Watch that tongue. It's like razor wire,' he marvelled, his eyes taunting.

'I want to ring my grandfather,' she told him coolly.

'That mercenary old man!' With black brows lowered in

a hard line above stony eyes, he scowled at her. 'Did you know that I never wanted to marry you, Maddy?'

She froze. There was an odd expression on his face as if he wished he hadn't said that. But the truth was out now.

'You rat!' she husked. It had only been lust, then.

His mouth twisted. 'Grandpa will be very disappointed in you.'

With an angry jerk of her head she stood her ground. 'He'll have no cause! I can tell him that you and your grandmother had no intention of any alliance. You wouldn't have married me if I'd been drop-dead gorgeous with ten million in the bank and a fluorescent halo!' she stormed. 'Do you know what I think? That you both wanted to humiliate Grandfather and me for reasons I don't understand—'

'No. That's not true.' He put down the glass and folded his arms decisively, leaning against the door jamb, his long legs crossed at the ankle. 'Grandmama wanted the marriage. She…she has reason to feel regret that she didn't support you and your grandfather. She genuinely felt sorry that he is in such poor health—'

'We don't want your pity!' she flared.

'You have it, nevertheless,' he said sternly. His eyes burned into hers. 'Both of you. I am sorry you've had a hard life. But that was no reason for me to let myself be trapped in a loveless marriage. I didn't want to marry you, Maddy. I don't want to marry anyone.'

'Feeling sorry for me didn't stop you from planning to seduce me from the start,' she began indignantly.

'That's not true, either. Not…to begin with, anyway. I swear on my mother's grave that initially I didn't want any involvement at all.'

'And…then you did,' she scathed. 'All that chest-to-chest dancing. Those sultry looks and the things you whispered in my ear—'

'I'm human. You were—are—very provocative.' When she eyed him doubtfully, he took a sip of his wine. And to her surprise, he said gruffly, 'Let me get you a glass. I think it's time to put the record straight.'

Perplexed, she followed him into the living room. Accepted the wine and sat down on the sofa. At least they were talking. There was so much she needed to know before she left. She cringed back into the deep cushions when he came to sit next to her but he leaned forwards, brooding over his own glass.

'Explain,' she prompted him coldly.

There was a tense pause. She watched him turning the glass in his hands, his lowered eyes intent on the swirling ruby liquid. Then he licked his lips and began to speak in a low, quiet tone that had her straining towards him to hear what he said.

'Since my arrival after the fire I have been trying to organise the rebuilding of the Quinta, as you know. I've been up to my neck in architects' plans, site visits, site clearance, temporary offices, obtaining and housing the seed and plant deliveries…' His hand swept back his hair in a gesture of impatience. 'And all the while I had nothing but an ear-battering from my grandmother about getting married and producing an heir.'

'I sympathise,' she muttered.

He grunted. 'I was particularly annoyed that she'd colluded with your grandfather and you, apparently offering me on a plate.' His mouth twisted wryly. 'My marital status is none of her business and I'd told her so, repeatedly. But she went ahead with this ridiculous scheme to marry me off. Consequently I was overjoyed when you turned up dressed unconventionally and behaving without any decorum whatsoever.'

Maddy detected a faint smile lurking at the corners of his mouth. 'Glad I delighted you,' she said sarcastically.

'More than you know,' he muttered under his breath. And whilst she was trying to work that out, he continued in a louder voice, 'As you know, Grandmama was appalled. I thought it would teach her a lesson if I pretended I was smitten.'

Her mouth opened and shut in astonishment.

'*What?* You...you were kidding all the time during that dinner?' she gasped.

He nodded. For a moment or two she stared at him and then she burst into laughter, which soon turned to hysterics.

'Oh,' she cried weakly, 'that's so funny!'

They'd both been frantic to keep each other at arm's length! If only they'd known at the time—the dinner would have been even funnier...

Weak with laughing, she collapsed and held her aching stomach, her eyes sparkling with humour.

'Oh, I hurt! It's priceless! The joke's on both of us, Dex,' she giggled. 'I never had any intention of marrying you either!'

'Yeah. And my name's Tinkerbell,' he said scathingly.

'Hi, Tinkerbell,' she chuckled.

His eyes simmered with indignation.

'You had that book. Something about snaring your man.'

'That's right,' she said cheerfully. 'Pick it up. Read it. See what it says,' she challenged. 'The instructions suggest that a prospective bride should dress conservatively. Be demure. Subservient, unquestioning. Agree with everything your prey says.' Her eyes danced merrily. 'Would you say that describes me?'

His mouth curled. 'Hardly.'

'There you are, then! I studied it—and did the opposite because the last thing I wanted was to snare you.'

'Sure. The moon's made of cheese.'

'No, don't you see?' she said in delight, leaning forwards, her hands hugging her knees. 'Grandfather went on and on at me as well, until I agreed to come here. But I wasn't ever going to marry you.'

'Why not?' he shot. 'You knew I was rich.'

'But the whole idea was loathsome to me!'

'Thanks.'

'No,' she said hastily. 'I mean the idea of marrying someone purely for money. So to please Grandpa but to stay single, I had this...' she laughed '...this cunning plan!'

The dazzling breadth of her smile bemused him. He passed a shaky hand over his fevered brow, trying to bring his mind to order. It could explain how mild-as-milk, bullied little Maddy had suddenly emerged as a man-eating hoyden.

'This...plan,' he said, huskily.

'Yes, Dex.'

She drew back, her eyes shining with a tenderness he'd never known before. Not since... He frowned ferociously. Luisa, he thought guiltily. But with Maddy there had been more. A depth he'd never experienced. Had it ever been that good with Luisa? Had he ever lost himself so completely and wondered if he'd died and gone to heaven?

He went cold. Because he hadn't.

'Plan,' he jerked, unable to say much more.

She let out a rich giggle. 'It was wonderful! I had so much fun, Dex! I bought some shocking clothes in charity shops, changed my hair colour and practised using make-up and walking with a wiggle. All I had to do then was be outrageous so that you and your grandmother would find me totally unsuitable. I practised on the rugby team and...'

her eyes slanted to his '…and a particularly gorgeous truck driver I met.'

He cleared his throat and sipped frantically at his wine.

'You played the part brilliantly,' he muttered, unsure.

'Did I?' she asked eagerly.

'*Unusually* well.'

'You're not convinced, are you?' she said gently.

'Is it any wonder? It would take quite an actress to pull that off.'

'No. Just desperation. Dex, I promise you, it wasn't that hard once I'd got a bit of confidence. Clothes make a difference, I promise you. People respond to you in a different way and you're halfway there. And…I do believe that inside me there's been this saucy minx waiting to get out all these years. I didn't like upsetting people, but it was a revelation to discover how enjoyable life could be. I really was Miss Meek-and-Drab until I set off for the airport. Ask my grandfather—anyone who knows me in England. Ring my friends. Ask for a description. You'll get "quiet", "reserved", "not interested in fashion". And probably, if any of my friends are honest enough, "downright dull, but harmless"!'

His glance shot sideways at her and he could feel a smile beginning to tip up the corners of his mouth. She'd been fabulous at that dinner. His body was leaping into life at the very memory of it.

'Do you mean to say,' he murmured, 'that all that slurping your soup and going on and on about shopping and money…that was an act?'

'Absolutely,' she said firmly. 'Cross my heart.'

'The wriggling snake?'

She blushed and giggled. 'A masterpiece, I'd say!'

He grinned, remembering.

'Mesmeric,' he agreed. 'That corset thing—'

'Basque.' Her eyes twinkled. 'I could hardly breathe in it. And I almost chickened out of wearing it, but I knew I had to make an impact of the wrong kind.'

'And how!' he breathed, lifting his eyes to heaven. 'Lap dancer, indeed!'

Maddy laughed in delight.

'To this day, I don't know how I came up with some of that stuff!'

'Well,' he murmured, 'at least I know that you haven't had any part of your body pierced.'

She went pink. 'I was treading on very thin ice sometimes,' she admitted shyly.

'I had a ball, skating along with you,' he drawled. He took her hand. 'Maddy, I believe you. And I'm glad you're not a money-grabbing little minx.'

Her beatific smile made his heart thump.

'It was fun pretending to be, though. Oh! That reminds me!' she cried, looking alarmed. 'I owe you a stack of money.' Before he could say anything, she was racing across the room towards the corridor. Returning, she pushed the wad of notes towards him, her face wreathed in smiles again. 'Thanks,' she said, sitting down again. 'It was a wonderful moment.'

'Why?' he asked wryly, putting it on the arm of the sofa.

'Seeing your horrified face and realising that I'd convinced you I was after you for your riches! And while we're about it,' she went on, mock-indignation in her tone, 'were you taking the mickey when you said I had hair the colour of rhubarb wine and the directness of a Roman road?'

He roared with laughter.

'Guilty! What an evening it was!'

'Oh, Dex!' she sighed. 'It's lovely to hear you laugh.'

'It feels good,' he admitted huskily. 'Thanks. Today was hell. You've made it bearable.'

'I'm so glad!' she whispered, and her hand tightened in his.

'You'll be going home soon, then?' he croaked.

Her gaze dropped and she seemed to be staring at her knees with unusual intensity. Then she looked at him and his heart began to pound furiously in his chest.

'In a little while. But I'm not sorry I came. All these years, Dex, I've been a timid mouse. I've let Grandpa have his own way too often. By wearing wacky clothes and being assertive I've found another person inside me. Oh, I'm still soft, and I'll probably still weep at old movies, but I've learnt the benefits of being more assertive. I have respect for myself now.' The warmth of her eyes intensified. 'And I'll never regret seeing Portugal again, or knowing you.'

'Is that...as in "knowing", or in the biblical sense?' he asked quietly.

Her smile made his heart leap.

'Both. Now,' she said with a patently false lightness of tone, 'time I rang Grandpa to say I'm on my way home.'

His hand stayed her.

'Don't go. Not yet,' he murmured softly.

'Why?' she breathed, not looking at him.

But her hands were shaking and he could feel the passion pouring from her voluptuous body. 'Because of this,' he whispered, bringing his mouth down on hers.

CHAPTER TEN

THEY made slow and languid love through the night, taking a delight in giving one another pleasure. Maddy didn't hold back. With Dexter she felt that she could do anything, say anything.

When she talked of her life with her grandfather he listened intently, as if he was fascinated, asking dozens of questions about the minutiae of her daily existence.

And so she told him in more detail about her work in the children's home and the sadness she felt when children arrived looking miserable and wary, then the joy that came when they began to laugh and fool around.

It was a night she would never forget. During it she realised with absolute certainty that she had fallen irrevocably in love with Dexter, every bone in her body and every ounce of flesh and blood alive and throbbing because of him.

Now and then, when she surfaced from his arms, a nagging little voice reminded her that this would only be a brief interlude in their lives. But she didn't care. An interlude was better than nothing at all. And so she pushed the little voice out of her mind and concentrated on more selfish, hedonistic needs for the first time ever.

'I rang my manager to tell him I'm taking the day off,' he told her eagerly, when they were eating an enormous breakfast late the next morning. 'What would you like to do?'

'Anything,' she said softly, 'if we can be together.'

He leant over and kissed her lingeringly on the lips. 'I

gave Manuel and the men the day off too,' he said. 'There's a rugby match on that they'd like to see—'

'Oh!' she cried in delight. 'Me too, if it's my friends from the plane! Can we?'

'If you promise to wear something outrageous and prance about knocking everyone dead,' he murmured. 'Can't disappoint them.'

Her eyes sparkled. 'I've got that outfit with the marabou trim—'

'Don't even *think* of it!' he growled in mock-anger.

She laughed, overjoyed that he should be jealous, even as a joke. 'You choose, then.'

His hungry glance fired her body. 'It'll take hours,' he said throatily. 'I'll take your clothes off and make love to you, then I'll dress you in some violently coloured piece of nonsense and take that off and make love to you, and then—'

'Talk!' she sniffed. 'Is that all you can do?'

She skipped away when he made a grab for her and she ended up being chased around the table and laughing so hard that she was an easy catch.

'You pay a forfeit,' he husked, nuzzling her neck.

'Oh, good!'

Her happy face lifted to his. Dexter's amused expression slowly melted and became serious.

'Maddy,' he said shakily. 'Did you tease all your boy-friends like this? Those social workers and doctors you spoke about?'

Her finger touched his anxious mouth and she stared at him solemnly.

'As I said, I had a few boyfriends,' she said quietly. 'But I was too reserved to tease them and they were intimidated by Grandpa. I...' She bit her lip. 'I never let the relationships get very far anyway.'

It hadn't been fair, either to herself or her boyfriends. How could she fall in love—and risk someone loving her—when she was barren?

She hesitated. Then decided to trust him. Not about her private secret, because there wasn't any point, but her experience. Her hand caressed his face lovingly.

'You haven't realised, have you?' she mused. 'My forays into sex only got as far as being kissed and slapping away the rare, occasional groping hand.'

'But…you're so good—'

'Am I?' She beamed. 'Learnt entirely from TV. Plus my instinctive responses. Until you, I was ignorant of lovemaking.' She smiled gently. 'I'm glad I was a virgin for you. I have the feeling that few men could have given me such pleasure.'

His eyes were moist. For a moment he gazed in bewilderment at her and then slowly his head lowered. She closed her eyes, surrendering to the extraordinary tenderness of his kiss.

How could she ever leave him? she wondered, as they walked hand in hand to the bedroom. He had her entire heart. Something had been awoken in her that would never be surpassed. A profound, undying love.

It was precious, she thought, blindly kissing him with a desperate frenzy. To be enjoyed to the full. For soon they would part.

And the hectic, fevered quality of their lovemaking suggested to her afterwards that he, too, knew it would be only a short episode in their lives. And he had every intention of living for the moment as well.

'The pink.'

'No!' she gurgled, sitting half-naked amid a sea of gaudy clothes. 'The tangerine cropped top and scarlet ra-ra skirt.

I intend to be seen across the entire rugby pitch and blind the opposition!'

'You'll do that all right,' he said with a grin. 'I'm wearing two pairs of sunglasses and carrying a riot shield if you go out in that.'

'Help me on with it,' she enticed, her eyes wickedly bright.

Dexter groaned. 'No,' he moaned, collapsing onto the much-used bed. 'Not again! Spare me, you insatiable wench!'

'I just like to feel your hands on my body,' she purred, stretching lazily.

He held her then. Very close, as if loath to ever let her go. It was a sublime moment for her. The whole world seemed to be on her side for a change, and determined that she should have her share of happiness.

Gently he kissed her neck and along a tingling line to her shoulder.

'Maddy,' he said huskily.

The breath caught in her throat. There was something about his tone that made her certain he was about to say something special. Like...*stay forever*. She bit her lip. Of course she couldn't. There was Grandpa, for a start.

'Yes, I know,' she breathed. 'Time to get dressed and go. Right,' she went on briskly. 'Find your own glad rags and I'll dive into mine. Race you.'

A flicker of disappointment briefly tightened the muscles of his face and then he was smiling.

'The winner gets to drive,' he said, and catapulted himself towards his own room.

With a squeal, Maddy flung on her top and skirt, pushed her feet into a pair of luminous pink trainers and got to the car keys on their hook in the kitchen a fraction of a second before he did.

Flushed and laughing, they tussled for a moment and then melted together in a long, warm kiss.

'You're wonderful,' Dex said in an appealingly husky croak.

Her rapturous face lifted to his. 'I know,' she agreed with a happy giggle.

Like two kids, they fooled around on their way to the car, arms around one another, doing a silly little dance.

Delighted to be driving such a beautiful car, she burst into song as they bowled along the road. Dexter sat with his arm around the back of her seat, his body relaxed with contentment.

She kept giving him rapid little glances, because she couldn't believe that they had become lovers—and friends. She sighed with the bliss of it all.

'Concentrate, sweetheart,' he said softly, his fingers lightly toying with a curl at the nape of her neck.

How could she? Though of course she must. But that term of affection meant everything to her.

'Dad used to call me sweetheart,' she said shakily.

A firm and comforting hand rested on her shoulder. Although Dex said nothing, she knew he understood how badly she missed her beloved father.

And she wished for the millionth time that she'd been able to build an affectionate relationship with her mother before she died.

'Not far now,' he said gently. 'Next turning left.'

Carefully she pulled off the main road and drove the sleek silver car to the pitch where the teams were already warming up.

'This is so exciting!' she cried eagerly, as they headed towards the players. 'Look! That's the boys! I wonder if they'll see me—'

'Are you kidding?' Dexter said ruefully, when a whoop

went up as 'the boys' recognised Maddy. 'No holding, no funny goings-on in the scrum, mind,' he warned with a grin.

'Maddy! You came!'

'Maddy!'

'Hi, gorgeous...'

She was surrounded. Hugged breathless, lifted in the air, kissed soundly on the cheek. Laughing and joshing, the players talked nineteen to the dozen to her, demanding to know what she'd been doing.

Even they'd be astonished if she said casually that she'd been busy falling in love, so she just said that she'd been having a cracking time.

'And this is Dexter—Dex! Where are you?' she cried, unable to see beyond the mass of men pressing in on her.

Without much difficulty, Dex shouldered his way through. Her eyes shone to see him. He was as tall as most of the men there. And, although he wasn't as beefy, his charismatic presence ensured that he looked stronger and more powerful than all of them.

He was clapped on the back and recognised as the Meeter and Greeter at the airport, a fact which made everyone chuckle and wink a lot. Dex began to talk with great interest about rugby and they all became engrossed in a discussion on tactics until the coach interrupted them and reminded them why they were there. Maddy tucked her arm in Dexter's and they settled to watch the match.

That evening Dex took Maddy and the team out to dinner in Luz. For her it was a bonus that the friendly, kind-hearted players should like and respect Dexter. Watching his manner with waiters and his staff, she realised that he was truly a good and considerate man. And he was her lover.

Gazing around at the table of laughing, chattering men,

Maddy felt so happy she could cry. Good food, good company, someone you love. What more could anyone want?

Perhaps a womb that worked, she reminded herself. And took a sip of wine to divert her mind. This brief encounter was enough for her. It really was. She would cherish it till the day she died.

For the rest of the week she and Dexter hardly left one another. They both rose early and set off together for the site, where she—at her own suggestion—began to organise the transport of seed and plants from his suppliers all around the world.

A small portable site office had been delivered, and it soon became the centre of all activity. Spread on a large map table in the office were the blueprints for the new Quinta, which was to be rebuilt with reclaimed old stone and roof tiles and traditionally carved arches over the doors and windows.

There were to be landscaped gardens and a huge new client car park, beautifully screened with palms and oleander. The nurseries would be watered with state-of-the-art technology and warehouses would store the pots and compost required for such an enormous undertaking. The concept took her breath away.

It worried her that he must be spiralling deeply into debt and facing financial ruin. Several times she began to bring the subject up, to suggest that he begin in a less ambitious way, but he always stopped her from expressing her doubts.

Everyone worked long hours, not least herself and Dexter. More and more she recognised the devotion of the men towards him. And her admiration for his even temper and his capacity for hard work and problem-solving grew day by day.

In his arms each night, she marvelled at his patience and

passion. It was as if no one else in the world existed for him but her. Every now and then she felt a pang of fear. She was getting in too deep. He had become the be-all and end-all of her life and parting would be an agony.

'I'm going to church this morning,' he confided when Sunday came around and they were lazing in bed. 'And then to my grandmother's for lunch. Would you like to come, or stay here?'

'What does she know about us?' she asked hesitantly.

He gave a short laugh. 'Only that we're here together. That was her idea, remember.'

'I imagine she's worried, wondering what's been happening,' she said, her face creased in an anxious frown. It wasn't nice deceiving Sofia, however unkind the woman had been to her.

'Possibly.' He kissed the tip of her nose and trailed a finger across her breast. 'On the other hand she might think I'm making use of you before I send you back home. You know the kind of girl you are,' he said with a grin.

'Right,' she said decisively. 'I'd like to come to church with you. And, yes. Lunch. But I want to tell her the truth.'

His wandering finger stilled. 'That you don't want to marry me?' he asked softly.

How could she lie? 'That my peculiar clothes and behaviour during that dinner were my way of making myself unacceptable,' she replied adroitly. 'I don't want her to think I'm really like that. And another thing. I'm wearing something demure of my own. I'm not walking into church with a bare tummy.'

'Good. I'm glad you're coming,' he said and kissed her so sweetly that she felt dizzy. 'I'll put some water on to heat for a wash; you make breakfast and put it in the warming oven till we're all pink and shining.'

It was, he thought, like being married. Or even better.

Maddy and Luisa were very different, but he had to admit that with Maddy he felt more vital, more full of fire and energy. Luisa had been balm to his tortured soul. Maddy had the ability to both soothe *and* arouse his senses. An extraordinary quality to possess.

And when she emerged later, dressed in a soft cream dress which flared from a fitted waist, he felt the breath catch in his throat.

'You are beautiful,' he said in wonder, his deep voice reverberating with emotion.

Sparkling-eyed, her mouth curved in shy delight, she blushed to the roots of her neatly combed hair.

'It's handmade and horribly ancient,' she demurred.

'Then it's you. Nothing to do with your clothes. And what's with this modesty?' he demanded. 'Where's the sassy woman I made love to last night?'

Maddy laughed. 'Oh, she's here!' she giggled. 'I do a chameleon act, didn't you know? And you look dishy in your suit,' she murmured, moving towards him admiringly. Her hand stroked his well-cut lapel and shaped to the contours of his chest. Then she looked up at him, happiness in every line of her lovely face. 'I'm having such a wonderful time,' she said shakily.

'Me too.'

He sounded husky. No wonder. His emotions were all over the place again. And when they'd parked in the small village square and walked quietly along the cobbled street to the small church he had an odd sensation that he would be content to live like this for the rest of his life: loving Maddy, working with her, attending church and family meals.

Simple things. But all the more enjoyable because she was with him.

'Dex!'

He turned at his grandmother's surprised call, exchanged smiles with Maddy and waited till the tall, puzzled figure had caught up with them.

'Grandmama,' he murmured, kissing her cheeks. He looked at her closely and saw with a pang of concern that she seemed thin and drawn. 'You remember Maddy, of course.'

'How do you do, Mrs Fitzgerald?' Maddy said gravely.

Sofia did a double take, then remembered her manners.

'How—how do you do?' she replied faintly.

'Maddy has said she would like to have lunch with us,' he said gently.

It occurred to him that his grandmother's look of alarm might have something to do with the fact that they always began Sunday lunch with soup. He stifled a grin and studied the shine on his shoes.

'Very well,' his grandmother said graciously. 'I'm pleased to see that Dexter has had some influence on your wardrobe, Maddy.'

'She—'

'I'm glad you approve,' Maddy broke in, interrupting his protest that her dress was not his doing.

'You look...quite acceptable,' Sofia said.

Seeing his grandmother's brain was whirling with possibilities, Dex crushed an amused smile and offered an arm to each of the women. They all walked into the little whitewashed church together.

'Oh, it's quite lovely!' whispered Maddy, awed by the colourful frescos.

Organ music—a piece by Bach, he thought—billowed around the bright interior, filling it with the sound of joy. All through the service, Dex felt a new serenity settling on him. As Maddy's incomparable voice soared rapturously to the rafters above, her face sweetly earnest, he sang with a deeper knowledge of human love than he'd ever known.

'You have a good voice,' Sofia said to Maddy when they were outside again, their heads reeling with the impassioned hallelujahs which had ended the final hymn.

'I'm in the church choir at home,' Maddy told her absently. 'And I teach Sunday school.'

'You?' Sofia blinked.

'Mmm. The parables are a particular favourite with the children,' she said, her expression soft and wistful. 'We act out stories like the Good Samaritan, and have a lot of fun strewing seed on stony ground and so on,' she added with a giggle. 'I'm highly skilled in turning loo rolls into shepherds and Magi, too.'

'Fancy!' was all she could say.

And for a while Dexter was speechless too. 'Before we have lunch,' he said eventually, 'Maddy has something to tell you. Why don't you both sit on the seat in the square, beneath the jacaranda trees, and I'll take a stroll?'

'Good idea.' Maddy took Sofia's arm and firmly marched her off to the square. 'Shall we?' she said politely, indicating the seat.

'What are you up to?' Sofia asked suspiciously.

'Nothing awful.' Maddy sat beside her and took a deep breath. 'I'm just putting the record straight,' she said, and explained the whole story.

When she'd finished, Sofia sat in stupefaction. 'You... you worked in a children's home? You're not brash and brassy and dedicated to shopping?'

Maddy laughed. She felt so much better for confessing. 'No! It doesn't go with my Sunday-school-teacher image!'

'You don't want to be a—a lap dancer?' Sofia squeaked.

'Heaven forbid! I did tell the truth about that—I had talked about it with my friends,' she said hastily. 'We all agreed we couldn't understand how people had the nerve to do the job.'

'And...forgive me, I have to ask...the soup?'

Maddy put her hand on Sofia's. To her surprise, she didn't snatch it away. 'I was trying very hard to make you all dislike me,' she pointed out earnestly.

'You succeeded,' Sofia said drily. 'I couldn't believe you could be so insensitive and—'

'Oh! Yes! I nearly forgot!' Maddy exclaimed, squeezing Sofia's hand in her concern. 'I didn't know about the fire. Grandpa hadn't told me or I wouldn't have come. And I certainly wouldn't have capered about so merrily, either. I'm awfully sorry. It must have been a dreadful experience. Please forgive me.'

Sofia's mouth pinched in. No, it was wavering. She was trying not to laugh! And now she was smiling...grinning... Oh, thank goodness! Maddy thought. She was laughing!

'You are a wicked girl,' Sofia reproved, but there was a wonderful twinkle in her eye. 'And very resourceful. I am impressed.' She beamed. 'I must say, I did feel invigorated by you that first evening. The atmosphere was like a mortuary until you breezed in. And then when you clapped the pianist so enthusiastically I wanted to join in. But my stupid, stubborn pride stopped me.' Sofia gave a low chuckle. 'Your dance set the whole place alight. I was terrified that Dex had fallen for you, hook, line and sinker!'

Maddy managed to keep her smile going. 'I did enjoy it,' she confessed. 'After a lifetime of being subdued and merging into the background, it felt wonderful to let rip.'

'Your grandfather keeps you on a tight rein,' Sofia said shrewdly.

'Bridled and blinkered,' Maddy replied with a rueful grimace. 'He's only trying to protect me, I know. It can't have been easy for him, being saddled with an eleven-year-old girl.'

'No.' Sofia averted her gaze.

'Tell me—' Maddy began, but she changed tack when Sofia tensed noticeably. She'd ask Dexter what had happened. 'Why did you and he want to marry us off to one another?' she queried instead.

'My dear, your grandfather and I are getting old. We worry about you both. He's afraid you won't be able to manage on your own. I am worried that Dexter will never settle down and will roam around the world for the rest of his life. He needs a wife and children.'

'Children,' Maddy said, choked.

'I thought that the gentle, sensitive little Maddy would be perfect.'

She blinked in surprise. 'Is that how you remember me?' she asked in astonishment.

Sofia's hand cradled Maddy's face in affection. 'As a wide-eyed, sweet child who adored the Quinta and everything in it,' she said softly. 'Oh, I know I was too strict with you. I'll never forgive myself. But with so little input from your mother, your father was letting you run wild, and I was afraid you'd turn into a hooligan.'

'I understand,' Maddy said.

'Dear child, to be so forgiving.' She sighed, her eyes misty. 'I was right in choosing you for Dex. I thought your care and concern for others would be just what he needs.' Her face cleared and she laughed in delight. 'That's why I was so shocked when you turned up in that red corset and began to set the hotel and everyone in it about its ears! Come on. Here he is. Let's have lunch, shall we? I want to hear all about your life in England.'

'Everything all right?' Dex asked cautiously when he reached them.

'Perfect,' said Sofia, beaming broadly.

But Maddy had to force her smile. Dex shouldn't be denied children. She wasn't right for him. Even though she loved him with every fibre of her being.

CHAPTER ELEVEN

THEY sat beside the hotel pool after a very harmonious lunch, drinking strong black coffee. After a while, Sofia drained her cup and gave a sigh.

'Time for my nap. All this chatting has exhausted me. No, you needn't accompany me to my room, Dex,' she scolded mildly as he and Maddy jumped to their feet. 'I know the way. I'm not decrepit yet.'

'I'm well aware of that, Grandmama,' he said with a wry smile.

'I'll see you again, Maddy,' Sofia said firmly.

'I'll be going back to England soon,' she said.

'Are you?' The old lady looked at her carefully as if weighing her up. 'That would be a shame.'

Maddy flushed, pleased that she had made her peace with Sofia.

'I'll see you before I go.'

'You certainly will!' Sofia said with spirit, and walked briskly away.

'She likes you,' Dexter mused.

Maddy smiled. 'And she adores *you*.'

He gave a small laugh. 'I think not.'

'She hangs on your every word. Besides, she told me so when you were ordering our coffees at the bar.'

'But... She's never said—!'

'She keeps her love deep inside,' Maddy said gently. 'I think she's been hurt and is afraid of your rejection. But she admires you and longs for you to live here. She's missed you desperately.'

He shook his head in disbelief.

'All I get is criticism—'

'I noticed that.' She put her hand on his arm and lifted her earnest face up to his. 'But she admitted that she wants you to be perfect. To make no mistakes. That way you'll suffer no setbacks or problems.'

'You're an extraordinary person, Maddy,' he said quietly.

She sighed, wishing she could be perfect for him. A whole woman.

'I have flaws, like everyone else.'

Dexter took her hand and held it tightly. 'This may sound like an odd invitation, but...would you like to visit the cemetery where your parents are buried?'

Her eyes widened in gratitude. 'I'd like that very much, Dex. Thank you. Thank you! I'd hoped to get there some time during this visit but I can't remember where the cemetery is. I was only eleven, you see, and when we drove there I was in floods of tears and Grandpa was growling at me to be quiet.'

His eyes were full of pity. Gently he stroked the nape of her neck.

'We'll go right away if you like,' he said gently. 'Your parents are buried at Bensafrim. Mine...are elsewhere.'

She gave a nervous laugh. Her lower lip quivered and he took her into his arms. Hugging him, she said chokily into his ear, 'Grandpa wouldn't tell me what happened. He just blurted out that my parents and yours had been in an accident and were dead. Every time I tried to ask him what had happened he got into a terrible state. He said talking about it all would never bring them back, so what was the point? I was frightened I'd lose him if I pushed for an answer. So I feel a huge part of my life is unaccounted for.'

'Then I must fill in the missing pieces for you,' he said huskily.

Bensafrim turned out to be a tiny little village a short distance to the north. They parked by a gate which she vaguely remembered and, carrying the flowers and the vase she'd bought with Dex's help, she walked with him into the tiny cemetery.

'Yes,' she said, clutching his hand very tightly. 'This is it. All these graves, those with railings around...the little chapel...and—and the wall all around with—with recesses for graves. I can't remember much else. I was crying non-stop.'

He squeezed her hand reassuringly and then put his arm around her shoulder.

'I'll help you look. Let's start by the chapel.'

The sun beat down on them. The whitewashed walls, about six or seven feet high, had the effect of keeping the pleasant breeze out. Consequently the atmosphere in the small cemetery seemed stifling.

'Here,' Dex said, a short distance ahead of her.

She took a deep breath. The marble which had been placed in front of recess number ninety-three was difficult to read because the black paint had worn off the carved letters. Trembling, she crouched down and peered at it.

'"In loving memory of James and Carlotta Cook,"' she whispered. Her father and her mother... '"So tragically taken." Oh, Dex, it's so sad!'

The date was only decipherable when she felt it with her fingers. She couldn't have seen it anyway, her eyes had become misty with tears.

'There's a tap by the gate,' Dex said gently. 'I'll take the vase and fill it for you.'

'Thanks.'

Numb, she stared at her parents' grave, thinking of the

sense of abandonment she'd felt when they'd died. And she wondered why Dex's parents had been buried elsewhere. She began to cry helplessly.

She'd never been able to unravel in her mind what must have happened. Or to come to terms with the fact that shortly before the accident her father had abandoned her by disappearing with another man's wife.

Tears streamed down her face. She stepped closer and clenched her fists.

'How could you?' she sobbed. 'How could you run off, intending never to see me again?'

'It wasn't like that, I promise,' Dex said huskily, wrapping her in his embrace.

She wept into his chest, her body heaving with misery. Was she destined never to be with the people she loved? she asked herself in a rare outburst of self-pity.

'Hush. Hush,' Dex soothed. 'It's all right. It really is.'

Patiently he waited until she was calmer, with only the occasional body-racking sob lurching through her body.

'Now,' he said, tenderly drying her eyes, 'I'll fix the vase in the brackets, you arrange the flowers, and then I'll tell you what happened. All right?'

'Yes.' She snuffled, aching because he was such a kind and caring man.

And he would belong to someone else one day. Would comfort another woman when she was upset. Make love...

A huge, shuddering sob wrenched its way out of her mouth in a wail of misery.

Deftly Dexter finished securing the vase, stuffed the flowers in anyhow and drew her firmly away to sit in the shade.

After this she would have to leave. Her teeth drove into her lower lip and she hugged Dexter tightly.

'Tell me,' she whispered, desperately unhappy.

His hand lightly caressed the silky crown of her head.

'I suppose it began with a mistake,' he said quietly. 'You probably remember that your mother was very beautiful?'

She searched her memory. 'Not really. I was too concerned with the fact that she didn't love me,' she mumbled.

'It wasn't that simple,' Dex said. 'You see, your father might have been madly in love with her at first, but the relationship was destined to fail.'

'Why?' she muttered.

'Because your mother adored cities and shopping and hated the countryside. She loathed the Quinta and became cold and dissatisfied. To be frank, she was something of a shrew and a nag.'

'Yes,' Maddy mumbled, a bitterness like gall in her throat. There had been rows. 'I remember now.'

'It wasn't her fault. Both of them had chosen badly. Misery can warp people's characters, sweetheart. Joy brings out the best in them.'

'True,' she said in a small voice, grateful for his understanding. She didn't want her mother to be the cruel, shrill woman she envisaged whenever she thought of her.

'My father was also disappointed,' Dex said quietly. 'In me. He'd wanted a tough, games-playing hero for a son, and he got a skinny runt with weak eyesight.'

'He was awful to you,' she said darkly.

'I'd ruined his dreams.'

'If only he could see you now—'

'Yes.'

She fell silent. There were too many 'if only's on the tip of her tongue.

'What about your mother?' she asked, lifting her head so that she could see his face.

And he smiled with such sweetness that she felt her heart lurch uncontrollably.

'She adored everyone. Saw good in them all. I don't think I could have survived without her. When I was quite small—seven or eight—she saw that I had a flair with plants and coaxed your father into letting me work with him.' He hesitated. 'I hated your father for years because I believed that he enticed my mother away from me and split our families asunder. Now I understand how the power of passion can carry you away. Of course they fell in love. They were twin souls. They couldn't help it because they were destined to be together. Both of them were unhappy, both of them were generous and kind with the same passions in life.'

'But they weren't together for long,' she whispered, her throat choked with tears. And she likened her father's brief moments of love with her own.

'No.' Dexter kissed her forehead and drew her deeper into the circle of his arms. 'It all went wrong when your father sent Mother a note, asking her to meet him on Yellowhouse Beach.'

'And?' she asked, hardly breathing.

Dex sighed. 'I was there when Grandmama found the note and showed it to my father. He told your mother and they went to the beach to confront the lovers. Apparently there was a terrible row.'

'I was fishing with a friend that day,' she remembered. When she'd returned, it had been to a terrible atmosphere. Her weeping grandfather had told her that her parents were dead. Soon after they'd packed their bags and left. Her head lifted and she looked at Dex. 'I didn't see you at all. Where were you?'

She felt every muscle in his body tighten. His grip was uncomfortable but she didn't say a word. Within the deep cavity of his chest, his heart had begun to thunder. She waited, patiently, apprehensively.

'I was in the garden, cutting—ironically—a split branch on the Judas tree. I could hear this peculiar revving of engines. Then two cars came careering up the narrow track towards me.'

'Our parents?' she hazarded.

His mouth was bitter. 'Yes. But not together. Your father was driving the first car, with my mother in the passenger seat. The others were following in hot pursuit.'

'Oh, Dex!' she breathed.

His voice grew very soft. 'I could hear your mother shouting, egging my father to overtake the first car. Their wheels touched. And they crashed.'

'You saw it!' she gasped in horror.

'I got to them before anyone else,' he agreed, his tone brittle and thin. 'Your father was still alive. Just. It was obvious that…that everyone else was dead. I went to him. He said…' His voice broke.

Maddy's eyes squeezed tight shut as she felt his pain. And visualised her beloved father. The tears streamed down her cheeks.

'Go on,' she begged.

Dex stroked her hair gently. 'He was desperate to tell me what they'd intended. You see, Maddy, he and my mother had been coming back for us. There had been an argument between them all, over who should have custody of you and me. My mother couldn't bear to be without me. Your father desperately wanted you. He said…he said, "Tell Maddy I love her with all my heart."' He bowed his head. 'But because your grandfather kept you away from me from that moment on I never got the chance.'

She cried as though her heart would break. And yet it was a cathartic release. Her father hadn't abandoned her after all. A huge weight had lifted from her shoulders.

Dexter's voice sounded soft and husky close to her ear.

'They died because they wanted us, Maddy. I can't tell you how I felt. Because she couldn't bear to be without me, my mother died. And for all these years I've felt a crucifying guilt. They could have slipped away and still be alive. Our parents would have divorced, but we would not have been deprived of them at such a young age. And—' he sighed '—I wouldn't have harboured such a terrible hatred towards my grandmother,' he added bitterly.

'Why would you hate her?' she asked, puzzled.

'Because she could have screwed up that note and let my mother handle her own life, instead of interfering. I know that Mother would have broken it gently to my father. She would have found a kind, less traumatic way of saying that she wasn't in love with him any more. Instead, he found out in the worst possible way. At the time, of course, I was beside myself with grief and shock. I told Grandmama that she'd as good as killed my mother with her own bare hands.'

'Oh, how awful for you both!' Maddy murmured in sympathy.

He sighed heavily. 'I must have hurt her badly. Your grandfather was furious with her, too. And he hated my mother for luring your father away, as he said at the time, with her wicked feminine wiles.'

Maddy eased herself from Dexter, her tears drying on her cheeks. He needed reassurance, and because she loved him she tried hard to find the right words.

'It was an accident,' she said gently, and it was her turn to stroke his frowning brow and to offer comfort. 'A tragic accident. Nothing else. You weren't to blame. You must know that now.'

'I always did, really,' he said in a low tone. 'But I still felt the guilt.'

She nodded and held his hand in hers. 'So you ran away.

You punished yourself,' she told him. 'And your grandmother.'

'I realise that,' he said quietly.

'She has very strong moral values. She must have been faced with an awful dilemma when she found that note. Don't blame her, Dex. Or yourself. We can console ourselves with the fact that each one of our parents must have loved us very much to have been so desperate to get to us first and claim custody.'

'Yes,' he said huskily. 'I suppose you're right. Thank you, Maddy.'

She was silent for a moment. And then, 'I'm glad I know everything now. There's just one thing that bothers me. I can't understand why my grandfather didn't tell me what had happened,' she said, frowning.

'You must ask him,' Dexter said in a gravelly voice thick with emotion. 'Perhaps he was too upset to speak of it. Old tyrant though he was, he genuinely adored your father more than anything and anyone in the world. And perhaps he felt he couldn't explain the facts to an eleven-year-old girl. The least said the better. He was never good with feelings, was he?'

She nodded, realising now that maybe her grandfather's cold, stern appearance had hidden a wealth of misery. He'd suffered greatly but he didn't know how to show emotion, it was true.

It was growing dark. She had what she'd come for. Stiffly they got up from the bench and made their way back to the car. On the silent journey back she thought of the tortured note in Dex's voice when he'd told her about the crash.

And when they arrived at the cottage they undressed by candlelight and went straight to bed, just hugging one another.

In the early hours, she woke to find that he was watching her. She shuddered at the tenderness in his eyes. His warm smile seemed to enfold her in its protection and she smiled hesitantly back, knowing this would be her last day.

Dexter began to drop tiny, feather-light kisses on her forehead. She closed her eyes and felt his mouth moving over her face, inch by inch, as if they had all the time in the world.

It seemed she was in a dream, a slowly building vortex of sensation, as his mouth and hands worked gentle, insistent magic on her flowering body.

I love you, she thought to herself, experiencing the deep and whisperingly tantalising luxury of the silky slide of his skin against hers.

Drawing in a long gasp of sheer indulgent delight, she almost blurted out the truth of her love when he kissed her breasts.

But she dared not because of the pain that would bring.

I will remember this for ever, she told herself. And touched every part of him. Kissed him all over. Smelt his skin, inhaling his glorious maleness, tasted him and grew delirious under the constant, murmured onslaught of his throaty voice which was describing how he felt when he touched her.

Almost in slow motion they united, taking every ounce of long-drawn-out pleasure in one another.

The tenderness of their loving blew her away. She was incoherent with love and pain and the sight of his beautiful face moist with tears. He kept her on the peak of ecstasy for so long that she thought her body would disintegrate. And then, with impassioned cries and deep, bone-shaking shudders, they gradually came to rest.

Sated, she lay without moving, her lashes wet and dark

as one or two silver droplets squeezed from her heavily lidded eyes.

'Maddy,' he whispered.

'Mmm,' was all she could manage.

'I want you to stay.'

If she'd had any energy whatsoever, she would have gasped and jerked up. However, she opened her eyes wide to see that he was perfectly serious. A terrible anguish careered unstoppably through her.

'I can't,' she grated. 'Grandpa.'

'Would he come here to live?' Dex asked gently.

'Like a shot!' she mumbled. 'He is miserable in England. Loves the warmth here. But—'

His finger pressed firmly on her lips, preventing her weary mouth from moving.

'And…would you marry me, Maddy?' he asked.

Stricken with terrible pain, she turned her head away, but he brought it back so that she was forced to look at his brightly gleaming eyes.

'Don't tease me,' she muttered. 'You said you didn't want to get married.'

'I know.' His arms enfolded her. 'You're tired. Forget what I said. Sleep.'

Forget! If she ever could! He'd joked about something that meant the world to her…to marry him…would be…it would…

Her exhausted brain and body gave up. And she fell into a deep, dreamless sleep.

The morning sun blazed into the bedroom, waking her and causing her to groan and put her head under the bedclothes.

'Coffee.'

Loathing the brisk sound of Dexter's voice, she shouted, 'Go away!' in a muffled tone.

The clothes were ruthlessly stripped away, leaving her naked and vulnerable, the warm sun giving her body a golden sheen.

'Coffee,' he said again, but this time he sounded decidedly shaky.

'Why?' she scowled, glaring at his denim-clad thighs.

'Because I want you alert and attentive,' he said bossily, hauling her up and patting pillows behind her like a demented nurse in a black and white war film.

'Why?' she mumbled limply.

'Drink.'

She looked at him suspiciously from under her sulkily lowered brows and took in the clean white T-shirt and general aura of someone who'd been washed and dressed for hours and intended everyone else to be perky too.

'There's arsenic in it?'

'Ambrosia,' he corrected with a grin. 'Now, get it down you or I'm coming at you with a nice enema.'

'Brute,' she muttered. But sipped the coffee. 'Yuck!' she rasped as the caffeine galvanised her bloodstream. 'How many spoons did you put in this?'

'I lost count,' he said airily. 'Finish.'

'I've finished, I've finished!' she protested.

'Marry me,' he said, fixing her solemnly with his molten-tar eyes.

Her heart lurched. Not again. He had no idea how cruel he was being.

'I can't!' she wailed in a cracked voice.

'Maddy.' He sat on the bed, his expression serious. 'Are you uncertain that I'm ready for commitment?'

'You said you didn't want to marry,' she reminded him croakily.

'Yes. That's what I want to explain. The reason I didn't

want to marry anyone was because I've been married before.'

The wind was taken out of her sails. A small 'Oh!' was all that emerged. There was a long silence. Eventually she broke it. 'Tell me about her,' she whispered.

He sucked in a long, ragged breath. 'Her name was Luisa,' he said softly. 'She was a gentle and sweet kind of person, just what I needed to soothe me. With her I felt calm, instead of ravaged by guilt and self-recrimination. Her placid nature eased my pain.'

'That's nice,' Maddy mumbled, fighting the hurt, the jealousy. She was glad that Dexter had found solace. And wished it had been her.

He shifted his position a little, his expression far-away. 'We married,' he said simply. 'Gradually the nightmare visions of the accident began to recede. I hunted plants and returned to a quiet and patient wife. When she became pregnant I thought I had everything I wanted. I'd lost my family—but I could create my own.'

Maddy listened, barely breathing. Something about his sad eyes told her that this would not end happily. She realised that she loved him so dearly that she wouldn't even have minded if he was still married if that gave him joy. But instinctively she knew the relationship had foundered. And her heart bled for him.

'Go on,' she whispered tenderly.

He took her hand. Turned it over. Stroked the care-worn palm and kissed it, his face infinitely sad. 'She caught dengue fever, Maddy. She died, taking our unborn child with her.'

'Oh, Dex!' She held him tightly, aching for him.

'The shock was too much for me,' he admitted. 'I went to pieces for a while. From then on I vowed not to love anyone ever again, because every time I did they were snatched from me. And it hurt too much. Nearly destroyed me. But my heart hasn't listened to my head,' he said with a rueful smile. 'You have brought me back to life again, Maddy. I have fallen in love with you so deeply that I know I will never claw my way back to sanity again. I have fought this every inch of the way but perhaps I was always searching for someone like you. Gentle and caring, knowing when to be silent—and vital and vivid, laughing and happy, dazzling the world and making it a brighter place. I want to father your children. I want us to be a family. This is a big thing for me to do, Maddy, to ask you to be my wife. Commitment is scary because it makes you vulnerable. But I think I have seen love in your eyes. Last night was too sweet and profound for your feelings to be anything else. So marry me, Maddy. I love you and I always will.'

She felt utterly tormented by the hope in his eyes. He had set his emotions free after years of restraint. And now she was going to deal him a bitter blow. Her pain for him was even deeper than her own.

'You…you want us to have children—' she began hesitantly, floundering for a way to let him down gently.

'Oh, yes!' he cried enthusiastically. 'A rugby team, don't you think?' He laughed. 'And a netball team to even things up. No one ever accused me of discrimination.'

There was a terrible silence which grew longer and longer. The tension between them seemed as taut as a drum.

'Maddy?' he croaked, his face slowly, horribly, sagging.

'I can't tell you how sorry I am,' she said in a hoarse whisper. 'I wouldn't hurt you for the world. I—I admire you. We…we've had such fun together…'

'But,' he growled harshly.

She swallowed back the lump of emotion, knowing she shouldn't drag this out any more.

'Forgive me. I won't marry you, Dex.'

His gasp ripped through her as if he'd slashed her with a knife. He dropped her hand.

'Because you think I'm not rich?' he asked in a malevolent snarl.

She winced, her stomach churning with nausea. Where did she start to explain? Should she? She hesitated. And then knew she had to tell him the truth. Even though they'd never be together, she didn't want him to think it was because she cared about money.

'Dex, I know you must be in debt,' she began gently.

But he had stormed from the room before she could say it didn't matter, it wasn't the lack of money at all. Stunned, she heard the door slam. The car screech into gear. The scream of a careless acceleration.

And then…silence.

CHAPTER TWELVE

ALL day she waited. But he didn't return. Afraid to leave the cottage in case he came back when she wasn't there, she hung around, unable to settle to anything.

The next morning she walked to the site, but no one had seen him. Her heart in her mouth, she hurried back, intending to pack her clothes and somehow get herself to the main road. Perhaps one of the men would take pity on her and give her a lift to the airport. There was no point in staying. No sense in painful goodbyes.

However, from the hill, she saw a strange car parked outside the cottage.

'Dex!' she whispered, her heart thudding, spirits soaring. She raced down the hill, panting and moaning in her desperation to see him, to explain...

And when she flung open the door, flushed and bright-eyed, her disappointment at seeing only Sofia was so keen that she had to clutch at her chest to ease the pain.

'Is Dex with you?' she cried frantically.

'No, he's... My dear! Whatever is the matter?'

'He's disappeared! We had a row and he—he—he's *gone*!' she sobbed, flinging herself into the older woman's arms. 'And I love him so much and I have to tell him *why* I can't marry him—'

'Slow down, slow down, Maddy!' Sofia cautioned affectionately.

'You must know where he is! Please tell me,' she begged. 'He's the whole world to me, but I can't be his wife. He has to see that and then he won't be so hurt—'

'Why can't you marry him, child?' Sofia asked in a soothing tone.

'Because I had an infection ten years ago and I can't have ch-ch-children!' Maddy wailed.

Behind her, the door closed very gently.

She whirled around, face swollen with tears, to see Dex. His eyes were very tender and loving and her heart seemed to break with misery.

'Maddy,' he reproached shakily, 'did you think I cared so little for you? I can't deny that I would love to have children. But it's you I want to marry. I want you above everything in the world.' His eyes softened at her confusion. 'And if you want to know why I came back, Grandmama persuaded me. I went to her with my tale of woe and raged up and down for a while before she asked me a simple question. Had I actually established why you wouldn't marry me? Because she thinks I'm poor, I told her. And she said that was rubbish and you didn't care about money. I've been such a fool!' he cried. 'I should have known that! But I was too wrapped up in my own aching heart. Now I discover that you were trying to protect me from a childless future. Well, I'll take you as you are.' He grinned lopsidedly. 'Flaws and all. They'll complement mine. So now I'm asking you again.' He knelt on the floor and looked up at her with melting hope. 'Please, Maddy. Make my life complete. Be my wife.'

Her knuckles went to her mouth and she couldn't speak. But the lights in her eyes danced.

'Well. What about that, Grandmama?' he murmured. 'I do believe she's lost for words.'

'You won't want a wife. You like travelling. Being independent,' Maddy pointed out breathily.

'That was then. This is now. I like it better here. I *love* it here. And we can go on trips. I can show you all the places I've seen. Take you to the national park on the Cocos Islands, the most beautiful place on earth. That would make a good place for a honeymoon.' He assumed a theatrical frown. 'I want an answer, wench! Say it. Say yes.'

She didn't hesitate. 'Yes, Dexter,' she breathed, her eyes shining. He whirled her into his arms and kissed her passionately. 'I really don't care if you're poor!' she declared, anxious to reassure him. 'We can build up the business together. I'll help you. And…we can have Grandpa to live with us, can't we?' she asked. 'He wouldn't be any trouble, honestly. I'd see to that—'

'From what you've said, I imagine he'll be a lot happier and more relaxed if he can live here,' Dexter said. 'He'll also be pleased that we're getting married. It's just what he wanted,' he said wickedly.

'He doesn't eat much,' she said in agitation. 'He won't be a financial burden—'

'Maddy, you made the assumption that the fire had destroyed the business,' Dexter said gently. 'And it has certainly curtailed a good part of our income. But we were insured and have huge resources and outlets across Europe and South America which keep the coffers full. In a year everything here will be back to normal. Perhaps sooner. You are about to become a rich woman.'

'Oh, dear!' she said in dismay, quite flustered by the thought.

Dexter laughed with delight and kissed her. 'Don't worry,' he said fondly. 'Keep on being yourself. That's all I want. Now, how do we break the news to your grandfather without giving him a heart attack?'

'Actually,' broke in Sofia's silvery tones, 'he's in the hotel. I invited him over for a holiday when I saw how things were going with you two. He got quite emotional when I told him about the stunt you pulled, Maddy.'

'Oh, crikey!' she gasped, her hand over her mouth in horror.

'Never heard him laugh so much in all my life,' Sofia said, making a discreet exit. 'Come and see us at the hotel when you've finished celebrating. Bye.'

Maddy and Dex gazed at one another and fell into fits of laughter.

'Shall we seal our engagement?' Dexter asked, waggling one eyebrow lasciviously.

Engaged! She laughed again. Carefully she rearranged her features into screen-goddess sensuality. 'If you want to see my etchings, walk this way, big boy,' she husked in a Mae West drawl.

And she swung her hips exaggeratedly as she sashayed to his bedroom.

'*This* way?' asked Dex innocently.

Casting a sultry glance over her shoulder, she collapsed in giggles. A solemn-faced Dex was attempting the wiggle too. And failing abysmally.

But he caught her in his arms and whirled her around until she was dizzy, and the kiss he gave her after was more than successful.

What a wonderful time they were going to have, she thought contentedly as she began to show him her etchings. A new life, a new beginning…

The world's bestselling romance series.

HARLEQUIN®
Presents

Seduction and Passion Guaranteed!

Mama Mia!

Harlequin Presents

They're tall, dark...and ready to marry!

Pick up the latest story in this great
new miniseries...*pronto!*

On Sale in May
THE FORCED MARRIAGE
by Sara Craven
#2320

Coming in June
MARRIAGE IN PERIL
by Miranda Lee
#2326

**Pick up a Harlequin Presents® novel and you will
enter a world of spine-tingling passion and
provocative, tantalizing romance!**

Available wherever Harlequin books are sold.

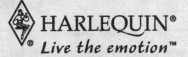

HARLEQUIN®
Live the emotion™

Visit us at www.eHarlequin.com   HPITHMA

eHARLEQUIN.com

For great romance books at great prices,
shop www.eHarlequin.com today!

GREAT BOOKS:
- **Extensive selection** of today's hottest
  books, including **current** releases,
  backlist titles and new **upcoming** books.
- **Favorite authors:** Nora Roberts,
  Debbie Macomber and more!

GREAT DEALS:
- **Save every day:** enjoy great savings
  and special online promotions.
- *Exclusive* **online offers:** FREE books,
  bargain outlet savings, special deals.

EASY SHOPPING:
- Easy, secure, **24-hour shopping** from the
  comfort of your own home.
- **Excerpts, reader recommendations**
  and our **Romance Legend** will help
  you choose!
- **Convenient shipping and
  payment methods.**

Shop online
at www.eHarlequin.com today!

INTBB2

If you enjoyed what you just read,
then we've got an offer you can't resist!

Take 2 bestselling
love stories FREE!
Plus get a FREE surprise gift!

Clip this page and mail it to Harlequin Reader Service®

IN U.S.A.	**IN CANADA**
3010 Walden Ave.	P.O. Box 609
P.O. Box 1867	Fort Erie, Ontario
Buffalo, N.Y. 14240-1867	L2A 5X3

YES! Please send me 2 free Harlequin Presents® novels and my free surprise gift. After receiving them, if I don't wish to receive anymore, I can return the shipping statement marked cancel. If I don't cancel, I will receive 6 brand-new novels every month, before they're available in stores! In the U.S.A., bill me at the bargain price of $3.57 plus 25¢ shipping & handling per book and applicable sales tax, if any*. In Canada, bill me at the bargain price of $4.24 plus 25¢ shipping & handling per book and applicable taxes**. That's the complete price and a savings of at least 10% off the cover prices—what a great deal! I understand that accepting the 2 free books and gift places me under no obligation ever to buy any books. I can always return a shipment and cancel at any time. Even if I never buy another book from Harlequin, the 2 free books and gift are mine to keep forever.

106 HDN DNTZ
306 HDN DNT2

Name	(PLEASE PRINT)	
Address	Apt.#	
City	State/Prov.	Zip/Postal Code

* Terms and prices subject to change without notice. Sales tax applicable in N.Y.
** Canadian residents will be charged applicable provincial taxes and GST.
 All orders subject to approval. Offer limited to one per household and not valid to current Harlequin Presents® subscribers.
® are registered trademarks of Harlequin Enterprises Limited.

PRES02   ©2001 Harlequin Enterprises Limited

June is the perfect month for a wedding!

So be sure to include our annual
celebration of romance and matrimony
in your reading plans....

the
Wedding
Chase

A brand-new anthology from
New York Times bestselling author

KASEY
MICHAELS

GAYLE WILSON   LYN STONE

The charm, wit and magic of
the romantic Regency period
come alive in these three
new novellas, each by a
top historical author!

Look for
THE WEDDING CHASE
in June 2003!

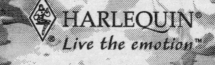

HARLEQUIN®

Live the emotion™

Visit us at www.eHarlequin.com

PHTWC

The world's bestselling romance series.

HARLEQUIN®
Presents

Seduction and Passion Guaranteed!

Coming soon from the internationally bestselling author

Penny Jordan

Arabian Nights

An enthralling new duet set in the desert kingdom of Zuran.

THE SHEIKH'S VIRGIN BRIDE

Petra is in Zuran to meet her grandfather—only to discover he's arranged for her to marry the rich, eligible Sheikh Rashid! Petra plans to ruin her own reputation so that he won't marry her—and asks Blaize, a gorgeous man at her hotel, to pose as her lover. Then she makes a chilling discovery: Blaize is none other than Sheikh Rashid himself!

On sale June, #2325

ONE NIGHT WITH THE SHEIKH

The attraction between Sheikh Xavier Al Agir and Mariella Sutton is instant and all-consuming. But as far as Mariella is concerned, this man is off-limits. Then a storm leaves her stranded at the sheikh's desert home and passion takes over. It's a night she will never forget....

On sale July, #2332

Pick up a Harlequin Presents® novel and you will enter a world of spine-tingling passion and provocative, tantalizing romance!

Available wherever Harlequin books are sold.

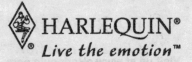

HARLEQUIN®
Live the emotion™

Visit us at www.eHarlequin.com

HPAN2

The world's bestselling romance series.

HARLEQUIN®
Presents

Seduction and Passion Guaranteed!

Back by popular demand...

EXPECTING

She's sexy, successful and PREGNANT!

Relax and enjoy our fabulous series about couples whose passion results in pregnancies...sometimes unexpected! Of course, the birth of a baby is always a joyful event, and we can guarantee that our characters will become besotted moms and dads—but what happened in those nine months before?

Share the surprises, emotions, drama and suspense as our parents-to-be come to terms with the prospect of bringing a new life into the world. All will discover that the business of making babies brings with it the most special love of all....

Our next arrival will be

**PREGNANCY OF CONVENIENCE
by Sandra Field**
On sale June, #2329

Pick up a Harlequin Presents® novel and you will enter a world of spine-tingling passion and provocative, tantalizing romance!

Available wherever Harlequin books are sold.

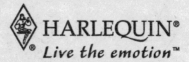

HARLEQUIN®
Live the emotion™

Visit us at www.eHarlequin.com

HPEXPJA